The Case of the
DOGNAPPED CAT

Books by Milly Howard

Brave the Wild Trail

Captive Treasure

On Yonder Mountain

The Case of the Dognapped Cat

The Case of the Sassy Parrot

The Mystery of Pelican Cove

The Runaway Princess

The Treasure of Pelican Cove

These Are My People

Milly Howard

The Case of the DOGNAPPED CAT

journeyforth®

Greenville, South Carolina

Library of Congress Cataloging-in-Publication Data

Howard, Milly.
  The case of the dognapped cat / Milly Howard; cover and illustrations by
Bruce Day.
    p, cm—(Pennant)
  "Crimebusters Inc."
  Summary: When neighborhood dogs begin to mysteriously disappear,
the newly-formed Crimebusters team takes on its first case and solves it
with the help of Samson, the huge tomcat.
    ISBN 0-89084-936-6 (pkb.)
    [1. Cats—Fiction.   2, Mystery and detective stories.] I. Day, Bruce,
ill. II. Title.   III. Title: Crimebusters Inc. IV. Series.
PZ7.H83385Cas 1998
[Fic]—dc20.   97-28148
                                                  CIP
                                                   AC

The Case of the Dognapped Cat

Edited by Debbie L. Parker

Illustrated by Bruce Day
Designed by Jamie Leong

© 1997 BJU Press
Greenville, South Carolina 29609
JourneyForth Books is a division of BJU Press.

Printed in the United States of America

ISBN 978-0-89084-936-1
eISBN 978-1-60682-996-7

25 24 23 22 21 20 19 18 17 16 15

To my sister, Helen,
who understands cats

Contents

Chapter One
The Old Desk

"I'm bored," Mark Conley said. He tossed his Atlanta Braves cap on the battered desk and ran his fingers through his dark hair. Slumping into a chair, he propped his feet up on the desk and sighed loudly.

"School's only been out two weeks," Corey said. He gently rubbed the braces on his teeth.

Mark sighed again.

"Besides, you can't be bored," Corey continued. "You've had one adventure or another cooking in your brain since we were in first grade."

"Not this time," Mark replied. "That last one did me in. I should have known a Mail Order *opportunity* would be a Mail Order hoax. If my folks hadn't loaned us fifty dollars, Sheriff Hadley said we'd have been in real trouble."

"Well, they did. And we earned every penny, too." Corey picked up a worn broom. "But the garage itself is clean, and if the loft is finished today, then the loan will be paid off. That is, if Maria Delores ever gets here. Where is she, anyway?" He took a few swipes at the floor with the broom. "She was supposed to be here thirty minutes ago."

"She'll be here," Mark said. He knew that nine-year-old Maria Delores Consuela O'Donnelly Ruiz could handle her end of adventure or work. "If she's late, there's a reason." He turned toward the ladder.

" 'Ol' yer 'races," a voice said. " 'M comin'!"

A mass of black curls appeared at the top of the ladder, and Maria Delores shook her hair out of her face, rattling the large paper bag she clenched between her teeth. She opened her mouth and let the bag fall on the loft boards. "I said, 'Hold your braces,' Corey," she said as he reached for the bag.

She used both hands to pull herself up the remaining few feet and swung her legs up into the loft. Sitting cross-legged, she gathered up the bag. "Ta-dah!" Maria Delores opened the bag with a flourish. The sweet scent of yeast rolls filled the air. "Sticky buns!"

"Ummm." Mark sniffed with appreciation. Then he hesitated. "Did you make these, Maria Delores?"

She frowned at him, but he wasn't sorry. Both he and Corey had been on the receiving end of Maria Delores's cooking experiments more often than Mark wanted to remember.

"Uh-uh," she replied. "From Aunt Lise."

"Oh, boy!" Corey exclaimed. Then he groaned, fingering the braces that kept him from eating sweets.

Mark had no such problems. He quickly wiped the dust off the desk. "You can put them here, Maria Delores," he said. He ignored Corey's woeful look.

"You can let one melt in your mouth, Corey," Maria said. "If you don't chew, maybe it won't stick to your braces." She took down the Thermos that hung from her shoulder. "And a drink will help."

Corey didn't hesitate. He hurried to the desk, trying to hand the broom to Maria. She just looked at him, one eyebrow raised. Corey picked out a roll and sighed, tucking the broom back under his arm. Mark chuckled. Maria had her own ideas about division of labor, he thought.

When the bag was empty, Mark went back to staring at the ceiling, occasionally licking his fingers.

"What's with him?" Maria Delores asked Corey.

"He's bored." Corey shrugged and began to sweep a little too hard. In minutes the dust had him leaning out of the loft window, coughing. When he could breathe without gasping, he pulled his head back inside the garage loft and glanced around, looking suspicious.

"I'll bet Samson has been sleeping up here," he said, frowning.

Mark knew that Corey's allergies got worse whenever a cat was around—especially Samson. But this time, Corey's sweeping had both him and Maria Delores sneezing too.

"It was just the dust," Mark gasped, fanning himself. "Nobody's been up here all year. Except for us, of course."

Maria Delores stumbled over the trash they had swept up beside the desk. She picked up a dusty sign that stuck out at an angle. "What's this?"

Mark swung around. He took the sign from her, rubbed off the dust, and held it up. *Crimebusters* was faintly visible against the dark wood.

"It's the Crimebusters sign," he said. "Dad told me he used to have a detective agency up here when he was a kid. I bet he left more stuff up here!"

He turned back to the desk and opened the center drawer. After scrounging around in the odds and ends, he found a yellowed notebook and a worn stub of a pencil. He flipped open the notebook.

"Hey, here's the record of his last stakeout! Listen to this—*9:10: cased Stanford's Grocery.*"

Maria Delores peered over his shoulder. "You mean he kept records and everything, just like a real private eye?"

"Yeah." Mark's boredom had disappeared. He grinned at Corey, who was leaning on the broom handle.

"Did he ever arrest anyone?" Maria Delores asked. Her dark eyes shone with interest.

"Um," Mark replied, lost in thought.

"Earth to Mark. Earth to Mark," Maria Delores chanted.

Mark ignored her. "Hey, just look at these notes. My dad never told me about this. He had real cases—people from all over town hired him to find

things. Here's a case about the Abbott pearls! These numbers at the bottom—Dad actually made *money!*"

"Uh-oh," Maria Delores said. She looked at Corey, a grin on her face. "Here we go again."

"We can start our own detective agency right here," Mark said, waving a hand. "Dad had the perfect place. Privacy for our clients, a desk, chairs . . ."

"Yeah, like who's going to climb that ladder to hire us? Can't you just see Mrs. Parsons climbing up here?" Maria giggled. "More like Tommy Ellis with a pocketful of pennies wanting us to find that ragged teddy bear his mother is always trying to lose."

Mark frowned at the mental image of the elegant Mrs. Parsons scrambling up the ladder. "We'll work something out."

He turned to Corey. "What do you think?"

Corey put down the broom. "You don't have to meet here . . ."

"Right! We can go to the clients," Maria Delores agreed. "We can advertise just like my uncle does. How about an introductory special?"

"Then it's settled? Maria Delores?" Mark asked.

"Count me in," she said.

"Corey?" Mark turned to his friend.

Corey hesitated only a second. "I'm in," he said. "But I don't see where—"

"Never mind! The three Crimebusters are open for business!" Mark said. He picked up the sign and hung it on a nail over the old desk. "Bring on the first case!"

Chapter Two
Samson

"*Rrrow.*" Inga Wolsiak's striped cat padded across the kitchen. He stretched lazily and rubbed against the door frame to ease the aches and pains still left from his last battle.

In the alley behind the house, evening shadows were deepening to dark purple. The cat's whiskers quivered. He sifted the scents drifting in through the screen door.

"*Rrrowww.*" He looked back at the elderly woman.

"Just a minute, Samson." She placed the last saucer in the dish drainer, then dried her hands on the kitchen towel. She picked up her cane and went to the door.

The cat twined around her leg. "We're a pair, aren't we, Samson?" she asked. "Now don't push us both over! You know I'm going to let you out. I always do, don't I?"

He waited silently. Then he slid through the crack before the door completely opened, as usual.

Mrs. Wolsiak chuckled. "Guess I'll not hear from you until morning." She closed the screen door and latched it. "Better get yourself home early, though," she called to the departing cat. "The Missions committee meets tomorrow morning, and I want to get there early to set up my display. You hear me, Samson?"

He stopped on the first step. He arched his back and limbered his muscles some more.

"Lot you care about me," she scolded fondly. "Just get yourself home safely." She turned away from the door, murmuring, "Now, where did I put that list?"

Samson meowed, sensing by her tone that she was no longer talking to him. Then he stalked down to the back yard. At the fence, he crouched for a minute, his tail lashing. The leap to the top cost him more effort than it had in the past. On the other side, he used the garbage cans to step down into the alley.

He spent the next half hour tracing the scent of each intruder who had dared enter the alley. When the alley passed inspection, he stepped out into the street.

He stood defiantly in the glow from the streetlight. His hair rose slightly along his back. Then he lifted his head and howled at the night. He waited, ready to defend his territory, but the night remained silent.

Satisfied, he turned left and padded down the block. The habits of years governed his route. At the first intersection, he crossed the street. He dodged the traffic with the ease of long experience. Only a battered, dark green van with muddy license plates had to swerve to avoid hitting him.

The driver leaned out of the window and shouted angrily. Samson stopped just long enough to give him a steady stare. Then he turned and continued on his route.

When he reached the Conleys' house, he scratched on the back door. The Conleys usually had a tidbit left from dinner that they saved just for him. Tonight was no exception. The door opened and Mark Conley appeared.

The boy wore pajamas, his dark hair still wet from the shower. "Okay, Samson, come and get it!" He dangled a big piece of shrimp for the cat. Samson took it gently in his jaws and lay down to bat it around. Mark sat down on the steps and watched until the cat finally finished the shrimp. Samson rubbed his nose against Mark's pajamas.

"Can't give you any more, old boy," Mark said. "Mrs. Wolsiak's orders."

He stroked the cat's thick back. "You're getting too fat as it is. Scavenging all across town is beginning to tell on you. Some young cat's going to take you out someday. You'd better watch it, you hear?"

Samson growled and stalked away, leaving the boy on the doorstep. As usual, he crossed the yard to the house behind Mark's and stopped below an open window. Then he lifted his head and let a high, wavering cry escape from his throat.

A startled face appeared at the window, braces gleaming in an open mouth. "Get out of here, Samson!" Corey's shout was followed by two loud sneezes. Then the window slammed down and the face disappeared. Samson rumbled softly, the sound deepening into a satisfied purr.

He cut across the Abbey Street cemetery and perched on a large, flat gravestone. Paw cleaning took about ten minutes. Then he crouched, ears alert, anticipating his next move.

At a quarter to ten, right on schedule, he headed for the Taylors' house. He eased through the hedge and covered the side yard in a series of dashes from shadow to shadow, belly almost to the grass. Near the back fence, he stopped, hesitating. Two unfamiliar shadows darkened the moonlit grass. Samson swished his tail and crouched lower.

"Think we put enough in?" a man's voice whispered.

"It's enough."

The other voice was lower, gruffer. Samson had a vague memory of a hoarse shout from a van. He flattened himself on the grass, ears back.

"When the stupid pug gobbles this meal," the second voice continued, "it'll be his last for a while. He will bring a good price in any market. Come on—while we're waiting, we'll check out the next street."

Samson waited until the man-noises faded. The two figures moved through the shrubbery and onto the sidewalk. Then the men, one taller than the other, slipped into a darkened van. The van moved quietly down the street.

Satisfied that danger was past, Samson continued on toward the Taylors' house. The fancy doghouse in the back yard was empty, and the overflowing food dish was unattended. Samson ignored the food and lay down to wait. After a while, the back door opened, and light from the kitchen poured into the yard. Blackenridge Prince the Third swaggered down the steps and across the grass.

"Nite-nite, Blackie," called Mrs. Taylor as she shut the door. The deep-jowled pug didn't look back. He trotted toward the food.

Samson waited until the pug was nose-deep in the bowl. Moving silently on the pads of his paws, he approached from the rear. He stopped a few inches from the dog and extended his claws, admiring their sharpness and length. Then he swiped the claws across the dog's exposed flank.

The pug yanked his nose out of the dish. He whipped around, teeth bared. When he found himself nose to nose with Samson, he cringed. Samson curled his lip in a silent snarl. The pug immediately gave way and scrambled for the back door, yelping all the way. The door opened quickly to admit him.

"Samson!" screeched Mrs. Taylor from the doorway. "Don't you eat all that food! I left enough for *both* of you. For shame!"

Mr. Taylor stood behind her, looking out. "Why you let that cat bully you is beyond me," he said. "He's blackmailing you, pure and simple."

"Well, I try to keep the peace with Samson," Mrs. Taylor replied. She picked up the shivering dog. "That cat gives him a case of the nerves."

"Humph," Mr. Taylor grunted. He turned back to the kitchen. "It's more a case of who's the cat and who's the dog. I think those two have their skins switched."

"Blackie's a show dog. He's worth hundreds of dollars," Mrs. Taylor said. "He's not a fighter."

"Not now, he isn't. Only pug I've ever seen that couldn't take care of himself." Mr. Taylor shook his head in disgust.

Now in full possession of the doghouse, Samson ate neatly and daintily. When he finished, he curled up inside. In a few minutes, he was fast asleep.

Thirty minutes later, the pug ventured outside again. Samson still slept. The dog slunk, tail between his legs, to the porch.

A green van cruised back along the darkened street. At the corner, the headlights dimmed and the engine stopped. The van coasted to a spot near the back fence. This time the men didn't talk. They moved silently toward the doghouse. One quick kick shoved the food dish out of the way. Another equally swift movement brought a sack down over the sleeping form in the doghouse.

Quickly, the men carried the sack back to the van, tossed it into the back, and started the engine. It purred quietly. At the corner, the men switched on the headlights and gunned the engine.

The sudden noise alerted the pug. He barked twice, then got up and trotted across the back yard.

He hurried to the dish and began to gobble the remaining food. When he finished, he yawned heavily. He entered the doghouse, sniffed out his violated territory, turned around twice and lay down. In a few minutes, he was sleeping soundly.

Chapter Three
Catnapped

Inside the van, Samson opened his eyes. He lay still, trying to get his bearings. Then he flexed his muscles and struggled to get up. Folds of rough cloth snared his paws and sent him crashing back down. He fell against something hard. The smell of raw gas sickened him, and he gagged miserably.

"What was that?" a man's thin voice asked.

A deep, gruff voice answered. "Jumpy tonight, aren't you?"

The other voice exclaimed, "Lay off, Mick! You almost got us caught this morning, going back for that stupid poodle!"

"Well, how was I supposed to know that poodle belonged to the police chief's wife?" Mick snarled. "If you'd been doing your research, that wouldn't have happened, would it?"

"I don't see why I'm the one to show myself in town." The thin voice went higher. "I take all the risks. I'm the one who talks to the customers. *My* face is the one they'll remember."

Mick's voice sounded more reasonable now. "But who will remember, Albert? You're the one who's got the knack of blending in with the background, right? And those big eyes of yours—they can melt the most suspicious heart in any town. Just remember that old battle-ax in Tallahassee. She still thinks you only meant to use her Scottie in a commercial. Last I heard, she had her nephew arrested for kidnapping the dog. You have a real gift."

"You're right," Albert said. "We couldn't make it without me. How about that lawn-mowing service I thought up? We check the houses for dogs while we're mowing, and the owners never suspect."

Mick sighed loudly. "Sure, Albert, sure."

Inside the sack, Samson made one more try to get up. He failed and sank back weakly. He lay still, waiting. The van floor vibrated gently under him. The sack slid a few inches backward and forward as the van stopped at traffic lights and accelerated again. It bounced slightly as the van rattled over the railroad tracks and turned.

For a long time, there was nothing except the smooth vibration of the engine. Samson drifted off to sleep once more. He awoke as the van turned, slowed, turned again, and bumped roughly along a side road.

Finally it stopped, and Samson drowsily tried to shift his body. Someone opened the door to the van. Samson caught a whiff of salty air, but before he could pull himself up, the door slammed shut and the van crawled forward.

"Get out and shut it," Mick growled.

"Look," Albert said. "I'm tired of climbing in and out to open and shut the dumb gate. What difference does it make anyway? It's not going to keep those dogs in. And who else would bother? Nobody's been here for ages."

"A deserted house attracts all kinds of visitors," Mick replied. "Especially a deserted house with electricity." He snorted. "Imagine Eldridge expecting us to camp out in the boondocks with gasoline lanterns and a propane stove! Anyway, I want us to be the only guests at this country inn. And I'm as tired as you are." His voice rose suddenly. "Got it?"

Albert answered quickly. "All right, Mick," he said. "All right."

The door opened again. When it slammed shut, the van accelerated and bounced up a short road. It stopped under a dense growth of pines.

Frantic barking filled the air. Samson stiffened in alarm. Before he could react, the door opened. Someone picked up the sack, jerking him upward. He fell back into the folds of cloth. His body hung heavily in space, and all he could do was spit.

The men clumped up something wooden. Steps? A door groaned. The sack swung as he was carried across a creaking floor. Samson's head buzzed. He moved in the sack.

"Where'll I put this one?" Albert asked over the noise of barking dogs.

Mick raised his voice. "Dump him in the room with the others!"

"You're crazy if you think I'm gonna open that door right now," Albert shouted back. "Those dogs would tear me apart!"

"That room down the hall," Mick said. "Put him there—just leave him in the sack. We'll take care of him in the morning."

"Suits me," Albert muttered. The sack swung some more as he walked down the hall. A minute later he dropped it on the floor.

Inside, Samson lay motionless, half stunned by the fall.

Someone pounded on the wall. "Shut up! Shut up, dogs!" The barking reached a fever pitch, then began to dwindle. Finally, only loud whuffling and an occasional bark could be heard.

Late that night, Samson began to gnaw at a rip in the seam of the sack. Every once in a while he had to stop for a rest, but he forced himself to keep working. Finally he chewed a hole in the rough cloth that was large enough to squeeze through.

He crouched on the floor. Dawn lit the room in a thin, gray light.

Samson yawned and stretched as he looked around, then he yawned again. He was alone here, but he could smell others in the house. Men. And dogs. Cautiously, he began to circle the room, staying close to the baseboards, detouring around the piles of old furniture.

The one window in the room was closed and boarded up from the outside. Samson leaped for the windowsill and fell back weakly. He tried again. This time he made it. He rubbed against the pane.

Early morning light poured around the broken boards. Through a crack he could see a tangle of palmettos and high grass that would offer him concealment if only he could reach it.

He pawed at the pane. It didn't give. He turned and eyed the open door. With one leap he was back on the floor. But something was moving in the other room. Bedsprings creaked.

Samson headed for a stack of chairs that leaned against one wall. Slowly, feeling more and more dizzy, he climbed to its height. At the top, he crept into the bottom of a broken chair and surveyed the room uneasily. Empty dog food bags lay crumpled just inside the door, and a few cardboard boxes were stacked against the opposite wall. Samson waited, his gaze fixed on the open door.

A faint scratching sound drew his attention to the ceiling. A small gray mouse was climbing into a jagged hole in the plaster.

Samson's stomach rumbled. He tensed, and the chair wobbled. In one desperate motion, he launched himself. His head and shoulders entered the opening, and he clawed the rest of the way through.

After he had breakfasted, Samson yawned. All he wanted to do was sleep. But first he had to explore his new territory. It lay above the rooms, covered by a sagging roof. Perhaps there was a hole in the roof that was big enough to squeeze through? No. There was no way out except down.

He tiptoed along the rafters, inspecting the fallen sections of ceiling. One rafter led into the room from which he had escaped. Another lay directly over the room behind it. Samson stopped on the rafter above this room and looked down. Most of the ceiling was gone, giving him a clear view. Dogs lay sprawled on the floor, sleeping. Samson's nose twitched, and he snarled softly.

Below him, one of the dogs woke and sniffed. It looked up. Suddenly a deafening roar of frantic

barking from all the dogs drowned every sound in the house. Samson crouched on the rafter, ears flattened.

The dogs ran in circles, throwing themselves against the wall in an effort to reach him. After a few minutes, Samson relaxed and draped himself across the rafter.

He watched drowsily as a brown spotted dog jumped again and again. After each effort, the dog fell back, panting heavily. Samson yawned. If the noise would stop, he could get some sleep.

Exasperated yells began to come from the front room. Samson remained where he was until footsteps stamped down the hall. Then he shrank back into the shadows to listen and watch.

"Knock it off!" Mick yelled, banging on the door.

When the dogs quieted, Mick stalked away, calling for Albert to bring the dog food. He stopped at the next doorway. There was a moment of silence as the man stared into the room where Albert had left the sack last night.

"Hey, Albert!" he called. "You put that pug in with the others?"

"No, I dumped him in the other room," Albert called. "You told me to!"

"Then where is he?"

"In the sack. Where else?"

Samson found a convenient rafter and settled down. Below him, a tall man appeared in the doorway, looking sleepy. He scratched his T-shirt and stared blankly at the empty sack in Mick's hand. "How'd he get out?" he asked in his thin voice.

"You should have dumped him in with the others," Mick said. "Now get cracking and find that pug."

Samson flattened himself against the rafter as Albert looked up. "You don't suppose he went up there, do you?"

Mick snorted in disgust. "A dog? What do you think he is, half cat?"

The men made a great deal of commotion with the piles of furniture, but Samson was too sleepy to watch. Finally they went away.

Samson closed his eyes.

Chapter Four
What's Up?

Mark sighed. "Well, maybe we'd better start hunting for that teddy bear of Tommy's," he said. "It's been an awful long time now."

"All those posters we handed out!" said Corey. "Didn't anyone read them?"

"Maybe our special was too cheap," Maria Delores suggested. "Nobody's taking us seriously."

Mark shot a rubber band across the room and opened the notebook again. "I wonder how Dad—"

"Someone's coming," Corey interrupted. He scrambled to his feet.

Mark hurried to the edge of the loft. Footsteps approached the garage. Then Mrs. Conley spoke from the open doors below. "There's someone here to see you, Mark. And you too, kids."

Mark grabbed the rope that hung from the garage rafters and swung down. He landed on his feet beside his mother. She flinched.

"If you miss, you'll land right on me," she said. "Why don't you use the ladder like Maria Delores and Corey?"

"Because I beat them to the rope," Mark replied. "What's up, Mom?"

"It's my Samson," old Mrs. Wolsiak said. She stepped inside beside Mrs. Conley. She leaned heavily on her cane. "He's gone."

"Come to think of it, I haven't seen him today either," Mark said, surprised. "I remember feeding him—oh, it was last night, wasn't it, Mom? That's when we had shrimp for supper."

His mother nodded. "We saved him a piece." She looked at Maria Delores and Corey. "You haven't seen him either?"

"Not lately," Corey said.

"I'm sorry, Inga," Mrs. Conley said. "Maybe the kids could ask around the neighborhood for you."

"Yes," Mark said. "We'd be glad to—The Crimebusters would, I mean."

His mother looked puzzled. "Crimebusters?"

Mrs. Wolsiak handed her a bright yellow paper. Mark recognized it as one of their posters. "Yes, the

Crimebusters. The grocery boy gave this flier to me when he brought my order." She smiled. "You know, I haven't heard that name since your daddy was about your age, Mark. Why, I remember the time he found an old sword that was stolen from the carriage house. And the time he discovered who was playing tricks on old man Evans. The minute I saw the poster, I knew I needed a Crimebuster just like your dad!"

"Crimebuster! My Jonathan?" Mrs. Conley sounded surprised.

Mrs. Wolsiak nodded, shifting her weight on the cane. "I always thought that experience with fighting crime as a youngster was responsible for his career in law, you know."

Mark grinned. He tucked a hand under Mrs. Wolsiak's elbow. "Why not discuss the details in comfort?"

The other two Crimebusters followed them back into the house. Mark controlled his impatience until his mother had settled Mrs. Wolsiak comfortably in the wing chair. Then he asked, "What makes you think Samson isn't just visiting around?"

"He always comes home." Mrs. Wolsiak's voice shook slightly. "He may roam at night, but early in the morning he scratches at the door. Or, in good weather, I'll find him sleeping on the porch. He never, never stays away for a long time. He knows how much I need him."

"So he hasn't come home since Monday night?" Mark tried for a professional tone. Maria Delores's eyebrows soared closer to her hairline, and her dark eyes sparkled with anticipation.

"No, this morning I had a meeting at church. He wasn't home by the time I had to leave," Mrs. Wolsiak replied. "I've never gone off without letting him in."

"You don't think someone took him, do you?" Mrs. Conley asked.

"Samson? Who'd want—" Corey began. A swift jab from Maria's elbow cut him off in midsentence.

"I doubt it," Mark said. "He probably just wandered off again."

"But he would have come back sometime," Mrs. Wolsiak said.

"Did you notify anyone? I mean, besides us?" Mark asked.

"Well, I called Pastor Jim and asked him to put a notice in this Sunday's bulletin. And yesterday I talked to Sheriff Hadley. He wasn't the least bit interested in helping me find him." Mrs. Wolsiak sniffed. "Said he was helping the Inglewood police chief on a case, and he didn't have time."

Mrs. Conley patted her shoulder. "It'll be all right, Inga," she said. "Samson will turn up, just you wait and see."

"But I thought—" Mark began.

"I'm not saying that you can't help, Mark," Mrs. Conley said. "I don't think anyone will mind if the Crimebusters return for a while."

"Yes!" Mark leaped to his feet, knocking over Mrs. Wolsiak's cane.

Maria Delores caught it, gave it a few baton twirls, and returned it to its owner with a flourish. Mrs. Wolsiak laughed shakily at their enthusiasm.

Mrs. Conley looked thoughtful for a minute. Then she said, "There are many people in our neighborhood and at church who have small problems that are unnoticed because they don't affect other people. They need help, and I think you three can give it to them. Helping other people shouldn't end up in the kind of trouble your last adventure did, anyway."

"You're right," Mark said. "When do we start?"

"We'll talk it over first with your dad, okay?" She smiled at him.

Mrs. Wolsiak put her handkerchief away. "And, of course, if you are allowed to search for Samson, and if you do find him for me, there will be a reward."

She stood slowly to her feet. "Since the sheriff couldn't help me, I placed an ad in the *Gazette* offering twenty-five dollars for information on Samson," she said. "I'll raise it to fifty if you can locate him for me."

Mark nodded, trying to listen and think at the same time. His mind was racing along the route that Samson followed every night. He reached for the pencil stub he had tucked into his pocket and opened his father's old notebook. Carefully he wrote *Case 1*. "Now, let's see, Mrs. Wolsiak. Samson comes by our house at about—"

Corey pulled a tissue from a pack he carried in his back pocket. He blew his nose and sank back into his chair. He grinned, and then he said, "Still bored, Mark?"

Chapter Five
Roadblock

"Crimebusters?" Mark's dad picked up the notebook from the kitchen table and thumbed through it. "I had forgotten all about this. Take a look, Margie."

"Yes, Mark showed it to me earlier," his wife said. "Now I know for sure that he got his sense of adventure from you."

Jonathan Conley handed the book back to his son. "We had a lot of fun before we disbanded it, anyway. What's this about?"

"We want to start up The Crimebusters again," Mark said eagerly. "We can make the loft into an office, just like you did. And we've already got our first case. How about it, Dad?"

"First case?"

"Mrs. Wolsiak's cat is missing," Mark's mother said.

His father laughed out loud. "Oh, how I remember—"

Then he grew more serious. "Now, if you accept cases, Son, you realize you have a responsibility to your clients?"

"Yes, sir!"

"Then welcome once again, Crimebusters!"

"Thanks, Dad!"

Mr. Conley smiled at the three friends. "Maria Delores, you keep these boys out of trouble, okay?"

She grinned. "Sure thing, Mr. Conley."

"Come on, let's get started," Mark said. He headed back up to the loft, deep in thought. Maria Delores and Corey followed.

"We've got to get into the suspect's mind," Mark told his partners. "And the best way to do that is to reenact the scene of the crime." He pulled out his casebook and leaned on the desk.

"But we don't have a suspect," Maria Delores said.

"Too bad you aren't a cat," Corey said. His braces glinted in a big smile.

"That's it!" Mark snapped his casebook shut. "You've done it again, Corey!"

"What?" Corey asked.

Mark caught hold of the rope. "Follow me, Crimebusters!"

As he pulled out of the driveway on his bike, he looked back. Maria Delores and Corey would catch up with him in a minute. They reached Mrs. Wolsiak's and parked their bikes at the alley entrance. Mark stopped to gather his thoughts.

"The only way to really *know* a cat is to *think* like a cat," he muttered. "Now, if I were Samson, what would I have done on Monday night?"

Corey stayed on his bike and pulled out a tissue to blow his nose. Maria Delores got off, but she leaned against a fence and watched Mark. Mark started down the alley, crouching low. He sniffed cautiously around the garbage cans and paused to look back.

"Come on, you two, get with it," he called.

Maria Delores looked at Corey and shrugged. "Come on, Corey," she said. "You have to get into it. You know, like a school play. Pretend that you are Samson." After stretching dramatically, she dropped to all fours and began to inspect the alley.

"No way." Corey sneezed and backed up his bike. "Meet you at the other end." He rode off before they could protest.

The other two continued their prowl through the alley. Mark applied everything he could remember about Samson's personality. He checked each garbage can. He even stopped at the back of the Harrison's fence to stare challengingly over at the terrier lying on the porch.

The terrier charged to his feet, his small body shaking with the yelps that erupted from his throat.

Mark clapped his hands to his ears. Maria Delores tapped him on the shoulder. "Look," she said. "I found him!"

Five feet away, a garbage lid teetered and crashed to the ground. A tail backed out of the can. It was followed by the haunches, shoulders, and head of a yellow cat. The cat swung around, looking for the yelping dog, and saw Mark and Maria Delores. Hissing, it dropped the fishtail it carried and streaked out of the alley.

"False alarm," Maria Delores said forlornly. "I thought we had him there."

"A stray," Mark said. "In Samson's territory."

Maria Delores looked at him. He knew what she was thinking. As far back as they could remember, no stray had dared enter this alley.

"Come on," Mark said, speaking a little roughly to hide his dismay. "Let's get back to work."

They crawled about on the ground for several minutes, but all they found was a rusted strip of metal and an old plastic bag that had fallen behind a garbage can.

"That's it, I guess," Mark said. "We just went down a blind alley."

Maria Delores giggled. "Well, it's not a total loss. I found out that I can do a better cat than you can," she said.

"Yeah? Watch this!"

Corey was standing by the fence. "Guys." His voice was quiet.

"Not now, Corey," Mark said impatiently. He did his best imitation of a cat stretching.

"Mark."

"Just a minute," Mark said. He tripped over a sneaker. "Watch it, Corey!"

"Watch it yourself, Conley."

Mark leaped up and found himself face to face with a tough-looking, blond boy.

"What's the matter, Conley?" The boy gave him a mocking grin. "Still playing Follow the Leader with your little friends?"

"I tried to warn you," Corey muttered.

"Well?" The boy's look was still challenging.

"We're on a case, Travis," Mark said. He tried to control the flush that he felt warming his face.

Travis opened the newspaper he was carrying. "Maybe a missing cat?"

"How did you know?" Mark stepped closer and glanced at the newspaper. "Oh."

"Oh, yes." Travis held it up so they could see the red-circled want ad. "It says a reward of twenty-five dollars here. A Mrs. Wolsiak. Now she wouldn't live around here, would she?"

"What makes you think—" Maria Delores looked angry.

Mark hushed her with a sweep of his arm. "Sure, Travis. She lives two houses down the alley. Have you found Samson?"

"Samson?" Travis's face was guarded.

"The cat."

"What if I have?" he replied.

"That's the case we're working on. Want to help?" Mark tried to sound polite, if not enthusiastic.

"Forget it." Travis stalked away in the direction Mark had pointed. Then he shouted back, "And forget about the cat, Conley. I've got it covered."

When he had disappeared from sight, Maria Delores straightened up, black eyes snapping. "Ay, yi, yi! That guy makes me—*furioso!*"

"Getting mad isn't the answer," Mark said.

"I know." Maria Delores looked sorry. "You don't suppose he has Samson, do you? Travis Burke lives out near the edge of town. As far as I know, Samson doesn't roam that far away from Mrs. Wolsiak."

"Who really knows how far that cat goes?" Corey said, sounding discouraged.

"Nobody, I guess—except the last one who sees him." Maria Delores started back down the alley. "Let's get our bikes. I'm not going to cat walk one more step, Mark Conley."

It took them until late afternoon to trace Samson to the Taylors' house.

"Monday night was the last night we saw him," Mrs. Taylor told Mark. "And I wouldn't care if he never comes back."

Corey laughed. "Why not?" he asked.

"That horrible cat chases my Blackie away from his food dish every night. I finally ended up putting food out for the both of them, but is that good enough for that domineering mistake for a cat?" Mrs. Taylor paused to take a breath. "Of course not! He takes it all and leaves my Blackie with no food and no bed. I've a good mind to call the animal shelter!"

"He ate here Monday night?" Mark carefully recorded the information in his casebook.

"Yes, and it serves him right too! Taking Blackie's food!"

Mark gave her a puzzled glance. "What serves him right?"

"Why, getting drugged, of course." Mrs. Taylor cuddled the pug close to her chest and stroked his head. "Poor Blackie."

She looked at Mark angrily. "That's what comes of having riffraff like that in the neighborhood. Someone got so mad at him they drugged my Blackie's dish, just to get at that cat!"

"Drugged?" Mark's eyebrows went up. He scribbled hastily.

"That's what the vet said. Tuesday morning we couldn't even wake Blackie up. He'd eaten it all, you see."

"All of what?"

"The rest of the food in the dish, of course. Blackie ate it."

"And it was really drugged?" Maria Delores asked.

"Yes, some sort of sleeping drug."

"Did the cat eat out of the dish?" asked Corey.

"I guess so," Mrs. Taylor replied. "He always did. Sometimes he only ate a mouthful, but he always took enough to aggravate Blackie."

"Maybe Samson got sleepy and was run over by a car." Corey's voice was not particularly gloomy.

"Maybe," Mark said. Thoughts whirled through his head. He wrote quickly and closed the book.

"We'll check back with you later, Mrs. Taylor. Maybe we'll have a line on the person who did this."

"I hope so," she said, stepping back into the house. "Who would think that something like this could happen in Boca Cay, of all places!"

They went down the sidewalk to their bikes. "Where now?" said Maria Delores. "We've reached a dead end."

Mark flinched. "Just a roadblock. Not a dead end."

"Well, we've already talked to Mr. Johnson, where Samson usually went next," said Maria Delores. "So Samson didn't go any farther than the Taylors' house."

"Then the trail does end here. It stops cold." Mark balanced on his bike. "A drugged dog. A missing cat. Come on, let's go."

"Hey!" Corey and Maria Delores spun off after him. "Where are we going?"

"To see Sheriff Hadley," Mark called back. "I want to know just what case he's working on!"

Chapter Six
Enemy Territory

Mark turned right at Main Street and headed for City Hall. About halfway down the block, he signaled Maria Delores and Corey to stop.

They braked beside him and balanced on their bikes, looking puzzled. He pointed toward the front of City Hall.

"There's Travis with Sheriff Hadley," Mark said. "What's he doing here?"

"Maybe he is working on this case," Maria Delores said. "If he is, he's one step ahead of us."

"Come on," Mark said, pushing off. "Let's find out."

The three stopped beside the sheriff and looked at Travis. "Hi, Travis," Mark said. "How's it going?"

Travis scowled at him and turned on his heel. He stalked away.

"What's the matter with him?" Mark asked. "What did I say?"

"He's just upset, Son," the sheriff replied. He slapped his hat absently against his leg. "He's lost a dog, too. That makes three in the last few days."

"Dogs?"

"Dogs. Looks like the dognappers that have been working in Broward County have moved their operation over here." Sheriff Hadley checked his watch and headed back up the steps. "Sorry, kids, but I need to make a call to the Sarasota police chief. See you around."

"Dognappers! Sheriff, wait a minute," Mark called. He parked his bike and ran up the steps beside the Sheriff. The others followed. "We need to talk to you."

"Make it quick," Sheriff Hadley said. "I'm short on time."

"Did you know Mrs. Taylor's pug was drugged? And that Samson is missing?" The pieces of the puzzle were beginning to fit together. "And that was Monday night?"

The sheriff stopped. "Uh-huh. I talked to Mrs. Taylor that night. Hysterical woman. And I heard about Samson. So what?"

"Well, if Samson ate some of the pug's food, he probably got drugged, see? And maybe the dog-nappers mistook him for the pug and kidnapped him, see? It all fits!" Mark tripped over a step in his excitement. "Don't you get it?"

Sheriff Hadley rubbed his graying hair and gave Mark an exasperated look. "Now what professional dognapper is going to mistake a cat for a dog? Even a cat like Samson?"

"Maybe they were in a hurry. Maybe it was too dark." Mark reached the door just as the sheriff opened it. "Who knows? But it could have happened, couldn't it?"

"Maybe. Maybe not." Sheriff Hadley paused, a frown adding another line of wrinkles on his forehead. "What are you kids up to, anyway?"

Mark stepped away from the door. Sheriff Hadley had not been at all happy with their "Mail Order opportunity." "We were just checking for Mrs. Wolsiak."

"Well, tell her not to worry." The sheriff slammed the screen door and started down the hall. "Samson'll come wandering back any day now!"

"Maybe," Mark said half to himself. "But as you said yourself, maybe not." He frowned. "If that sleeping drug was meant for dogs, it could really knock out a cat—maybe permanently."

"What would the dognappers do with Samson, anyway?" Maria Delores asked. "He'd be of no use to them."

"Yeah," Corey agreed. "He wouldn't bring ten cents at a flea market."

"So they'd get rid of him," Mark said. "The only question is, how?"

Corey broke the silence. "Well, what now?"

"We need to know more about the dognappers." Mark took out his notebook and flipped the pages. "We know that they drugged Blackie. But do they operate the same way each time? Or do they change? They seem to be slick characters. Maybe we ought to interview someone who actually lost a dog."

"You mean Travis." Maria Delores frowned. "Do we have to?"

"We have to," Mark said firmly.

"I don't have much time," Corey said quickly. "Got to help Aunt Caroline—she's throwing a party tomorrow."

"And I have to baby-sit tonight," Maria Delores added.

Mark knew that neither of them wanted to cross into Travis's home territory. "It's broad daylight," he said. "What could they do to us?"

"I could think of several things," Corey muttered. "Travis and his friends protect their territory like Samson protects his alley."

"Come on, Corey," Maria Delores said, trying to push her hair behind her ears. "If we don't go with him, he'll go off on his own. And Travis'll really like that."

The three Crimebusters rode east on Tarkington Drive. The summer sun warmed the shirts on their backs. Perspiration made their handgrips slippery. When they turned down Larkspur, dust trailed from their bike wheels.

They bumped across the railroad tracks onto Edgewood Trail, a potholed road that wound past a row of deserted warehouses.

"You feel it?" Maria Delores asked.

"The eyes." Corey looked back. "We're being watched."

Mark glanced back to see a figure run over the roof of a building they had just passed. Was the lookout signaling to someone hidden in the warehouse just ahead?

"The road's narrowing up ahead," he said quietly, slowing down. "And there's that old fence. That's where they'll stop us."

"We could've telephoned," Corey said with a groan.

They swung around a bend. Their way was blocked by five or six boys ranging from nine to thirteen years old. The boys formed a ragged line across the road. Mark stopped first, with Corey and Maria Delores close behind.

The silent boys had no weapons, nor did they make any move other than to block the way.

"Where's Travis?" Mark asked.

One of the older boys spoke. "What's it to you?"

"I want to talk to him."

"You and who else?" The boy looked pointedly at Corey and Maria Delores.

"Tell him Mark Conley wants to see him. These are my partners—Corey and Maria Delores. It's about his dog."

"Tell him yourself." The boy responded to an unseen signal and stepped aside.

Travis moved out of the shadows into the sunlight. "What about my dog? Did you see him?"

"No," Mark admitted, "but we're after the dognappers. We think they took Samson too."

"Okay, Conley," said Travis. "Come on."

His friends let Mark and Corey through, but one boy stepped in front of Maria Delores. "No girls allowed."

Maria Delores bristled. Her mass of curls seemed to bush out even farther around her hot face. "You are definitely *loco* if you think I'm staying out here!"

"Maria Delores is one of us," Mark said firmly. "Let her through."

The boy looked at Travis.

"She can come," Travis said.

Maria Delores pushed her bike toward the boy. "Take care of this for me, please." She walked past him, head held high.

Mark grinned at the boy's outraged look, then turned to follow Travis. He led them into one of the deserted warehouses. In a back room, a rough office had been made from abandoned tables and chairs. Travis waved toward one of the chairs. "Sit down."

Mark lowered himself into the wobbly chair. "Sheriff Hadley said you lost a dog. What kind was it?"

Travis frowned. "A setter. Purebred. Surprised?"

Mark stared at him, puzzled. "Why would I be surprised?"

Travis shrugged. "My aunt gave him to me two years ago."

"And he was stolen just recently?" Mark asked.

"Last night. Somebody slid in and snatched him without a sound. No struggle. Nothing. Skeeter just wasn't there the next morning."

"Did you check his food dish?" Maria Delores asked.

Travis gave her a sharp look. "Sure. It was empty, same as usual. Say, what is this, anyway? What business is it of yours?"

"No one saw anything? Heard anything?"

"I told you once—no!"

Mark looked around at the group of boys. "You guys keep track of your neighborhood. Did you see anything unusual that night? Any strangers?"

One of the boys nodded. "Yeah, come to think of it. There was a green van cruisin' about nine. I saw it on St. Mark about nine-thirty, and later on Linden, just cruisin'."

Mark's hopes rose. "Did you see anyone in it?"

The boy shook his head. "It was dark."

"What did the van look like?"

"Dark green. Muddy. Like a hundred others. So what?" the boy asked.

"Hey!" Travis interrupted. "No more questions. Just beat it, you hear?"

"We're trying to help," Mark said. "If we could just join forces—"

"Not likely." Travis's scowl was back in place. "You've used up your time. And this is *our* clubhouse. Move on."

Mark turned and led his friends to the door. "Have it your way."

"Hey!" The boy who had mentioned the van shouted after them. "I just remembered. The van had something about a lawn-mowing service written on it."

Mark turned back. "Could you read what it said?"

The guy shrugged. "I said the truck was muddy."

"Thanks anyway," Mark said. "That's a help." He tried to look casual as he got on his bike. Maria Delores and Corey rode beside him. Behind them, he knew, Travis's friends stood silently, watching. When the bend hid them from sight, Mark pedaled faster.

But Corey pedaled even faster. He shot into the lead. "Let's get out of here," he said. "This place gives me the creeps!"

Chapter Seven
Trapped

Samson opened one eye, then the other. He was hungry. He must have slept for a long time, but he felt stronger now.

He eased himself off the rafter to the edge of the broken ceiling. Furniture lay scattered all over the floor of the room below him. Those men had torn down the stack of chairs too. He couldn't get down that way anymore.

For a long time, he paced back and forth along the rafters. The dogs in the other room had been fed. Again they lay asleep on the filthy floor. Samson sniffed hopefully, but not one scrap of food had been left in the overturned bowls.

Silently, he returned to his perch. He would wait. Perhaps he'd take a nap.

The wonderful smell of fish awoke him. He lay perfectly still, testing the air. Fried fish . . . maybe an hour ago . . . on the other side of the house. He stood and stretched, getting each muscle ready for action. His stomach tightened, and his nose quivered.

He crept toward the broken ceiling above the empty room and listened. He heard nothing except the restless movements of sleeping dogs on the other side of the wall. On silent paws he reached the hole and peered over its ragged edge. Someone had thrown an old mattress against a chest. Carefully, he measured the distance, then hunger drove him beyond caution, and he leaped.

He hit the mattress with all claws out and flexed. They caught in the fabric of the mattress and held until his weight began to pull him down. The rotten fabric tore in long gashes, slitting the mattress from top to bottom. Samson landed on the floor, breathless but unhurt.

A dog barked uneasily in the next room, and Samson waited until quiet settled again. He padded cautiously out into the hall and stopped to sniff the air, whiskers quivering. Then he crossed the hall and entered the front room. It was deserted, and the front door was closed.

A slight breeze ruffled his thick fur. Samson checked the windows. The top sash was lowered just enough to let in fresh air. The crack was too small for even a smaller cat to get through, so he ignored it and headed toward the source of the tantalizing odor.

He paused at the kitchen door. The two men must have eaten the fish in here. But there wasn't even a scrap of garbage in the kitchen pail. Samson leaped from a kitchen chair to the table, then to the slanted counter.

A dripping faucet provided him with a refreshing drink. When he had finished, he inspected the sagging cabinets. A few pats assured him that the cabinet doors had the same worn latches as Mrs. Wolsiak's. He used his swat-and-bat routine on the first cabinet. Its door swung open, and Samson slipped inside.

Nothing but stacks of canned goods. He thrust his large body through the stacks to reach the back and sent the first row of cans tumbling out of the cabinet. They hit the counter and rolled off. In the back room the dogs began to bark furiously. Samson scrambled to free himself from the rolling cans. He sideswiped a plastic two-liter bottle of soda. It hit the floor and bounced twice.

The barking rose to a frenzied pitch. Annoyed, Samson screeched at the yelping dogs. Then he leaped down to the counter and swatted at another cabinet door.

These shelves were full of flour, noodles, and cereal. In his efforts to climb inside the crowded cabinet, Samson's claws caught in the paper bag of flour. He slipped and crashed down onto the counter, sliding sideways along its uneven surface. The bag of flour flipped over his head and hit the floor near the soda bottle. A cloud of flour rose into the air, and the loose cap blew off the bottle of already fizzing soda.

Samson leaped frantically at the noise. He slid along the rounded top of the ancient refrigerator and fell. When his clawing front legs hit the handle, he hung on until his weight pulled the handle down and dropped him to the floor.

The refrigerator's latch had been weakened by age. The door swung open by itself, revealing the contents of its rusty shelves. The sagging floor kept it from swinging shut again.

Samson lost all interest in the mess behind him as he inspected the contents of the refrigerator. A fish was on a platter near the front. It came off easily.

The spray from the soda bottle had stopped by the time he finished eating. He yawned and looked around to find a place to sleep off his meal. A basket of dirty laundry had been dropped beside the back door. He stepped lightly around the mess on the floor. When he reached the basket, he burrowed into the clothes. He was fast asleep in a matter of minutes.

At the sound of a door opening, he lifted one battered ear. But nothing was going to force him out of his comfortable cocoon. The now-familiar yipping and banging against the door of the dogs' room didn't bother him in the least.

"Put this one in the room down the hall and block the door," Mick said. "We won't take any chances with it."

"I still can't figure out where that pug went," Albert said. He started down the hall. "I tell you there was something funny about that. There was simply no way out of here."

"None that we know of," Mick said impatiently. He rubbed at his stained mustache and followed Albert down the hall. "Don't make mountains out of molehills."

Albert dumped the sack on the floor of the empty room. He froze when he saw the mattress.

"Mick . . ." His voice rose ending in a squeak. "Mick!"

"What's the matter now?"

Albert pointed to the ripped mattress, his finger shaking. "Look at that! Somebody's been in here with a knife!"

Mick stared at the room. He walked across the floor and inspected the mattress carefully. It looked as if it had been slashed repeatedly with a razor-sharp knife. "Check the house," he ordered. "Check every room!"

"You check it," Albert said. "You're the big guy."

Mick looked at him in disgust. "How I ever got hooked up with a wimp like you is more than I can figure."

He pulled a gun from the holster under his arm. "Here, will this put some backbone in you?"

Albert took the gun, and Mick ripped a leg off an old chair. "You keep the safety on that gun until we see something," Mick warned. "I don't want to be shot in the back."

When Mick stopped short in the kitchen doorway, Albert lurched into him. "The kitchen," he shrieked. "Look!"

"I'm looking, I'm looking!" Mick said. "Something or someone's been in here, that's for sure. What a mess! If they'd wanted something to eat, you'd think they'd just take it. This looks like the work of a—"

"A crazy." Albert's voice sank to a whisper. "Who'd think that a hick town like this would have crazies roaming the streets? Let's take the dogs and get out of here, Mick. Tonight."

"No." Mick's voice held more anger than fear. "Nobody's gonna run me off. Get a flashlight and give me that gun. We'll check the attic."

"The attic?" Albert's voice was shaky.

"Yeah. Now get going."

Mick pulled down the attic ladder. He climbed up and raised his head cautiously above the level of the floor. Albert closed his eyes, swallowing hard.

"There's nothing here," Mick said.

Albert breathed a sigh of relief. "Then he's done his work and gone."

Mick backed down. "Through locked doors?"

Panic returned to Albert's round blue eyes. "It's not a *he?* And *it's* still here?"

"Maybe. Maybe not." Mick shrugged. "We'll take turns on watch tonight. If there is someone here, he can't stay still forever. Clean up this mess and let's hit the sack. I'll take first watch."

Albert started to push the ladder back up. Mick stopped him.

"Leave it down," he said. "If anyone climbs that ladder tonight, he'll be stuck up there. Then we'll get him."

It took a while to clean the kitchen. When Albert finished, he found that Mick had set up the cots in the empty room.

"No way," Albert said, backing away. "I'm not sleeping in there. That pug clean disappeared from this room, and that mattress has razor marks in it. No way!"

"Fine," Mick said. "I can watch the stairs from here. You sleep on the couch."

"Sleep in the front room alone?"

"Alone," Mick snapped.

Albert went back to the front room, trailing a blanket behind him. He looked back once, but Mick showed no signs of changing his mind.

"Mick?"

"What now?"

"Can I have the gun?"

"Take it if it makes you feel any better."

Albert took the gun and settled down on the couch. After a few minutes he got up and turned off the lights. He clambered quickly back onto the couch and sat bolt upright, staring into the darkness.

Time ticked by, and the night noises diminished to a murmur. The house was quiet and still.

In the front room, Albert tossed on the couch, drifting in and out of an uneasy sleep.

In the empty room, Mick lay on a cot, eyes fixed on the ladder in the hall, the flashlight in his hand.

And in the kitchen, Samson crawled out from under the clothes and stretched.

Chapter Eight
Hands Up!

Samson padded lightly through the silent house. In the front room, he stopped to stare at the couch. He crouched slightly, his fur rising as he gazed at the covered form on the couch. A series of snores startled him. His thick muscles bunched under his heavy coat of fur. A rumble began in his throat.

A particularly loud snore shattered the quiet. Samson scrambled back against the doorway into the kitchen. He took up a fighting stance and answered the snore with the high, keening wail of his battle cry.

The snores stopped abruptly. Albert sprang to his feet, and the dogs began to bark.

"Whazat? Whazat?" he screeched into the darkness.

"Calm down, Albert," Mick yelled over the noise. "I'm coming!"

Confused by the sounds that came from every direction, Samson backed into the kitchen. His throat vibrated as he let loose another warning howl.

"Get away!" Albert screamed. "I've got a gun!"

"No! Don't—" Mick's yell was cut short by the sound of a gunshot.

Samson's claws screeched on the kitchen floor. Loud thumps pounded in his ears. A second later, a floor-rattling thud came from the hall.

Samson leaped across the kitchen floor and dived into the basket of clothes. He crouched at the bottom, every muscle tensed. His ears flattened against his head as he bared his teeth in a soundless snarl.

"Don't shoot!" Mick exclaimed. "Don't shoot! Put down that gun, Albert! Put it down!"

When no sound came from Albert, Mick carefully untangled himself from the ladder in the hallway. He crawled the few feet along the wall to the light switch, muttering as he crunched over broken bits of plaster. Cautiously, he stretched out one hand and scrabbled along the shattered plaster until he found the switch. The switch clicked, but no light came on.

Mick groaned and crawled back down the hall. He searched on the floor by the ladder until he finally found the flashlight. Then he pulled himself up and switched it on. He stopped in the doorway and stared around the front room.

Albert lay face down and sprawled across the floor. His bare feet were tangled in the bed sheet. The floor was littered with bits of broken plaster that had shattered when the bullet hit the wall between the front room and the hall. The gun was nowhere to be seen.

Mick sighed heavily. He stooped over and pulled up Albert's head by the hair. When he found nothing wrong but a bump on the forehead, he let the hair go. Albert's head hit the floor dully.

After searching the room, he found the gun. It had hit the floor and slid under a chair near the hallway. Mick picked it up and clicked on the safety. He scowled down at Albert. "Never, never will you ever get your hands on a gun again."

He started for the kitchen, picking his way carefully on bare feet. The kitchen was quiet, the back door still locked, and the windows were latched. Mick came back and bent over Albert.

"Wake up," he snapped. "Come on, get up."

Albert struggled to his knees, blinking. Mick helped him back onto the couch where he sat staring blankly across the room.

Mick grunted in disgust. "I can see I'll get no help from you." He shook Albert sharply. "Pull yourself together!"

When Albert finally focused on Mick's face, Mick said, "I'm going outside to check around the house. You keep watch here."

Albert nodded, but he didn't move an inch.

Mick sighed and unlocked the front door. "Not that I'll hear a thing over those yelping hounds," he muttered. "Shut up, there!"

The dogs quieted somewhat, and Mick stepped outside. He left the front door open to let the moonlight in. Then he moved silently along the porch. His heavy frame threw a giant shadow on the wall of the house.

At the edge of the porch, he stepped down onto the bare ground. He stifled an exclamation as he tripped over a tangled root. Limping, he followed the outside wall of the house around to the back.

He heard a scurrying sound at the back door. Quickly he released the safety on the gun. He pointed the flashlight toward the garbage cans and aimed the gun.

"Come out with your hands up!" he yelled.

A garbage lid sailed into the air and clattered down the steps.

Mick shot quickly, pulling the trigger three times before he charged the garbage cans. A big raccoon sprang from behind one can and headed for the thick underbrush behind the house.

Unable to stop, Mick dived over the cans and landed in the dirt. The rocking cans tumbled over on him, covering him with coffee grounds and soggy noodles.

Inside, Samson panicked at the sound of the clatter. He launched himself out of the laundry basket. On his way through the layers of clothes, his head poked through the neck of one of Albert's white shirts.

Albert was still sitting on the couch. When he saw the shifting white form sail through the air, he beat Samson through the door by mere seconds. As he crashed through the underbrush, he shrieked for his partner.

Just as frightened, Samson headed in the opposite direction. The first stretch of wild briars ripped the strangling shirt from his head. Relieved of its hampering folds, the big cat found the road. Tail straight out, hair on end, Samson ran for home.

Chapter Nine
The Stakeout

Mark snapped his casebook closed and sat up. He swung his feet down from the desk and faced the other two.

"I hate to admit it," he said, "but I'm stumped. We've interviewed every person in town who's lost a dog since this dognapping started. And what have we got? Zero. Zilch."

"At least we know the guys operate the same way each time," Maria Delores said. "They case the place some way, then they snatch the dog at night. They can't go on without running into some kind of trouble."

"Yeah," Corey chimed in. "Boca Cay is a small town. Somebody's bound to see them, sooner or later."

Mark got up and paced back and forth across the loft. He stopped to stare out the window. "It's too early in the morning for a case like this."

Corey yawned and stretched. "Too bad we can't run a stakeout ourselves on this one."

Mark blinked. "A stakeout."

He whipped around to stare at Corey. "A stakeout!"

Corey sat up. "What'd I do? What'd I say?"

"That's it," Mark exclaimed. "We'll stake out a dog, one that the dognappers wouldn't be able to resist! Then we'll grab them in the act of snatching a dog!"

Maria Delores thought for a minute. "Uh-huh," she said finally. "It just might work. But where are we going to get a dog? I don't have a dog. You don't have a dog."

Both turned to stare at Corey.

"Oh, no," he said hastily, backing toward the ladder. "Not Cinnamon."

"It's only for one night," Mark pleaded. "And just think how the headlines will read. *Crimebusters Catch Crooks.* How's that for starters?"

"*Aunt Caroline Crushes Corey* is more likely," Corey said. "No way. Besides, that Lhasa apso is beside her day and night."

"Corey, isn't there any way you could borrow Cinnamon?" Mark pleaded. "Just for a few hours?"

Corey shrugged. "Well—"

"Come on, Corey. Help out here," Maria Delores said. "We're running out of time."

"Well, Aunt Caroline is having her party tonight, and she asked me to . . ." Corey flinched. ". . . to sit for the dog."

Mark pounded him on the back. "That's it," he said. "That's it, Corey!"

Corey hiccupped nervously.

"All you have to do is bring Cinnamon over for a few hours," said Mark. "We'll set up a stakeout right here and rig it up so that not even a weasel could get in and out."

"We'll get them this time for sure!" said Maria Delores.

"How?" Corey asked simply.

"Come on; we'll plan it out." Mark pulled out a large used sheet of poster paper and half a ruler. Carefully he sketched his house, the garage, and the stretch of lawn in between.

"We'll tie her out here," he said, jabbing at a spot midway between the house and the garage. "We'll station Corey in the bushes here, just back of the dog."

He thought a minute. "And Maria Delores'll take a spot just inside the screened porch. I'll be here in the garage."

"What about your folks?" Corey asked.

"They always go to your aunt's parties," Mark said. "So do your folks. We'll ask if you can sleep over."

"Won't they be mad?"

"Why should they? We're home, aren't we? What could go wrong?"

Corey sighed.

"Well . . . what makes you think the dognappers will even come by?" Maria Delores asked.

Mark thought for a moment. "I don't suppose we could put posters around town—"

"Advertise?" Corey glared at Mark. "Not a chance!"

"Well, then, we'll try something else if they don't show up," Mark said. "Cheer up, Corey. Everything's going to be fine."

"So how are we going to stop them from taking Cinnamon?" Corey asked.

Mark smiled. "We're going to make a citizen's arrest."

"Citizen's arrest? Us? But we're just kids," Maria Delores said.

"Right. But we won't sound like kids. At least, one of us won't. Maria Delores, remember the voice changer you used in that skit you did last April? Didn't you get it from *Dynamic Electronics*?"

"Well, yes. Uncle Ramon lent it to me."

"Can you get it again in a hurry?" Mark asked.

"If he still has it," Maria Delores replied. "I'll check. He's got some other neat things, too."

"Okay. See what you can find." Mark turned to Corey. "Remember that old siren you've got in your basement? Think your folks will let us borrow it?"

Corey nodded. "Sure."

"Hey, where do we put this stuff when we get it?" Maria Delores asked, pausing on her way out the door.

"On the desk in the loft," Mark said as he stepped off the ladder. "Come on, Corey. Let's go!"

By late afternoon, everything had been gathered and stored in the loft, including a few extra gizmos Maria had not been able to resist.

The stack of equipment consisted of a parabolic mike complete with earphones, two sets of speakers and another microphone, a portable siren, and two sets of handcuffs that Maria Delores had bartered from a kid down the street.

"These handcuffs cost me five baseball cards and a torn baseball," Maria Delores said, snapping the cuffs on her wrists. "Best trade I ever made. No key, though."

"Hey . . ." Corey started toward her.

Maria Delores grinned and turned her hands down. The cuffs slid off and hit the floor. "Cuffs for grownups, right?"

Corey laughed. "Guess kids' cuffs wouldn't work. "

Mark picked up the parabolic mike. "Your uncle really let you have all this?"

"You know I didn't take it without permission," Maria Delores replied. "But he did tell me exactly what would happen if I didn't return it in the same condition it is now. So be careful."

Mark put the mike down gently and looked through the rest of the stack. "Where's the voice changer? Didn't you get it?"

"Well, yes . . ." Maria Delores hesitated. "I got it."

Mark looked at her, puzzled.

"It came with Julio attached."

"Julio?" Mark thought a moment. "Isn't that your cousin?"

"Yeah," Corey interrupted. "The one who pasted the stamps from my entire collection on his overnight case. No way!"

"He was only six when he did that," Maria Delores said. "Aunt Connie had just come back from Europe, and he wanted his suitcase to look like hers. He's much older now."

"How old?" asked Mark.

"Seven," Maria replied. "Uncle Ramon told him he could help us."

Mark sighed. "Maybe it'll be okay."

After thinking hard about the problem of Julio, Mark finally made up his mind. That evening he gave Julio a script and had Maria Delores coach him, using the voice changer. Satisfied that even Julio's voice could sound commanding with the proper equipment, Mark stationed him in the loft window, with a mike and the voice changer. "Now if you see anybody—and I mean anybody—come near that dog, you follow that script. Do you hear me, Julio?"

Julio nodded, pulling up his chair and clutching the mike stand with both hands. Mark started toward the ladder. He stopped. "Don't forget the voice changer."

Julio nodded again. "I won't, Mark. I promise."

Mark swung himself onto the ladder. Halfway down, a thought occurred to him. He scrambled back up and raised his head above the level of the loft. "And, Julio . . ."

Julio jumped. "What? What?"

"Don't you move one inch," Mark warned. "I don't want to see you, or hear you, or even smell you . . ."

"Okay, *okay.*" Julio hooked his legs around the chair and sat up tensely.

Mark sighed and climbed down the ladder. By seven o'clock, the bikes had been concealed in the garage, Cinnamon had been staked out, and Maria Delores and Corey had manned their stations.

Mark clipped on the earphones. He aimed the mike at Cinnamon. It picked up every jingle of her jeweled dog tag and relayed her every snuffle and whuff. To check the range of the mike, he aimed it at the bushes. He grinned as it picked up a sharp, crackling noise. He waited a moment.

The crackling was followed by a chewing sound. Corey was eating candy. *Hope it's not chocolate,* Mark thought. *Can't have him going allergic on us.*

He swept the mike around to cover the screened porch. For a moment he was puzzled by what he heard. Then he realized that Maria Delores was sitting in the porch swing. It squeaked gently as it swayed back and forth. Satisfied, he clicked off the mike.

He stepped outside to recheck the positions of the four speakers. One had been stationed on each corner of the garage. Two had been attached to the back of the porch. Then he climbed the ladder to the loft. It took a bit of persuasion to get the microphone away from Julio.

"I'm giving it back, Julio," Mark said. "I just want to check the speakers!"

Julio released his death grip on the mike and sat back just enough to let Mark reach it. Mark leaned over and whistled softly. Down on the lawn, Cinnamon broke into hysterical barking. Corey's head shot up over the concealing bushes, a startled expression on his face. Even Maria Delores pressed her nose to the screen door.

"Just checking, guys," Mark whispered hastily. The other Crimebusters gave him *all right* signals. They disappeared back to their stations. Mark squeezed back past Julio.

"You keep your eyes on that window," Mark warned. "And don't be moving around up here. You'll attract attention."

"Okay, okay!" Julio pushed his glasses back up on his nose. He grabbed the mike and pulled it out of Mark's reach.

For one brief moment, Mark thought about calling Julio's mother and asking her to take him home. But then Maria Delores would hear from Uncle Ramon and they'd lose the voice changer too. He shrugged. It was too late to change things now. He climbed back down the ladder and took up his position by the open garage door.

Time ticked by slowly.

Moonlight silvered the yard, spotlighting the silky-haired Cinnamon on the sweep of bare grass. For over an hour, she tugged nervously at the leash. Finally, she gave up and settled down to nap. Mark checked the loft window but didn't see any movement at Julio's station. Satisfied, he relaxed and made himself comfortable.

Lights went off in the neighborhood one by one. Only the golden glow of the streetlight was left to compete with the moonlight. Even Mark had begun to yawn, when Cinnamon sat up.

Mark straightened and followed her gaze. For a moment he thought the dog was simply spooking at nothing. Then moonlight glinted off a bit of chrome, and he saw it.

The green van was cruising with its lights off. Its dark color blended with the hedge on the other side of the street. Mark aimed the mike toward the open window of the van.

A thin, high-pitched voice came through the speakers so clearly that Mark winced. "She said something about a sitter this afternoon. The dog must be around here somewhere. Hey, Mick! Isn't that the dog?"

"Looks like her. But who'd leave a dog like that tied out? Especially when they're gone?" The other voice was lower, gruffer.

"Maybe the kid forgot to take her in," was the answer. "She's a beaut, isn't she? Look at that coat—and the way she holds her head!"

"Yeah, she's worth every inch of that lawn we mowed three times before it passed inspection. It's a good thing you heard the old lady ask the kid to sit for the dog."

A lawn care service! Mark thought. He took a deep breath and almost forgot to let it out. So that's it! They mow the lawns and case the place for dogs to sell!

He shifted the mike toward the screen door. It picked up Maria Delores's steady breathing. She was ready and waiting.

Good, Mark thought. He swung the mike toward the bushes to check on Corey.

Corey's breath sounded like it was coming in ragged gasps. Mark frowned. Should have frisked Corey for that chocolate before he went to his hiding place. Too late now.

Mark tapped on the ladder behind him to alert Julio. Then he turned his attention back to the men. The van had stopped, but the motor was still running. Both men got out and looked up and down the street. Then the taller one ran lightly across the grass. The other got back into the van and eased it along the street until it was directly across from Cinnamon.

Mark held his breath, waiting for Julio to start the script. Nothing happened. The man had reached Cinnamon and was unsnapping the leash.

Where was Julio? What had happened to the siren? The man picked up the unresisting dog.

Mark scrambled up the ladder. Julio lay face down on the desk, snoring lightly.

"Julio!" Mark hissed at him from between clenched teeth.

The boy jumped and blinked at him. Mark gestured wildly.

Julio looked down at the yard. Mark scrambled the rest of the way to the window and pointed. The tall man was heading back to the van, holding his hand over Cinnamon's muzzle.

Julio grabbed the mike instead of the voice changer. He threw open the channels to all four speakers. "S-s-sands up," he stuttered in his own voice. "We've got you hurrounded!"

On cue, Maria Delores and Corey switched on their flashlights. Mark reached over Julio and belatedly hit the siren switch.

Unfortunately, the man on the lawn was nowhere near the center of the trap. Mark snatched the voice changer from the desk. He pushed the button for the speaker nearest the fleeing man and yelled into the changer, "Drop that dog!"

The amplified, spookily vibrating voice boomed right in the man's ear. Mark caught a glimpse of a white face just before the man dropped the dog. Then the man covered the last few steps to the van door in a flying leap. The van accelerated and skidded around the corner. Cinnamon fled across the street into the vacant lot, yelping.

By the time Mark got there, Corey was wheezing. "I told you—" he gasped between gulps of air, "I told you—"

"Settle down, Corey," Mark said, helping his friend back into the garage. "We'll get her. I promise."

It took Maria Delores and Mark the better part of an hour to coax Cinnamon out of the tangle of briars and dead grass in the lot. Panting, they carried her across to Corey. Then they tried to pull out some of the burrs that had caught in her long hair.

Corey was still sitting in the open doorway of the garage. He watched them without moving.

Maria Delores looked at Mark blankly. "What went wrong?" she asked. "What happened to Julio?"

"He went to sleep on us," Mark said between gritted teeth. "Just wait until I get my hands on him. Where is he anyway?"

Corey took one look at Cinnamon's coat and shuddered. "Julio said to tell you that he doesn't want to play this game anymore," Corey said. "He took his voice changer and went home."

Chapter Ten
Travis

The sun had just begun to warm the sidewalks when Samson made it back into town. His shaggy hair was thickly covered with white dust. He loped along the street, head held low.

Travis passed the cat without giving him a second look. Then, near the corner, he stopped his bike and glanced back. There weren't any other cats in Boca Cay as big as Samson.

The cat padded toward him. Travis reached down to stop him, and Samson snarled.

"Huh." Travis grinned, jerking his hand away. "You look like you've had a couple of bad days."

Travis pedaled along behind the cat for a few minutes, thinking. Then he wheeled away and rode back to the corner market. He tried to keep an eye on the cat's progress while waiting in line to buy one can of EasyOpen Kitty Dinner. When the clerk finally rang up the sale, Travis snatched up the can and hurried after the cat.

He pulled the tab, stripping the lid from the can, and put it down for the cat. Samson ate hungrily, glancing up from time to time. Travis talked to him. By the time the can was empty, Samson was yawning. He didn't seem to mind when Travis picked him up and put him into the wire basket on the back of his bike. Travis took him to the warehouse office and settled him on a scrap of rug in the corner. Samson barely opened his eyes to curl up. When the other boys gathered in the office, he was sound asleep.

"Is that a cat?" one of the boys asked.

"It's the one we've been looking for," Travis said. "And if Mark Conley is right, he can lead us to the dognappers. We can catch the crooks, get my dog back, and turn them over to the police."

"How are you gonna get that cat to take you to the dognappers?"

"Take a look at him. Where do you think he's been?" Travis asked.

"Down a shell road," one boy said. "He's covered with white dust."

"How far down?"

"How would we know that?" the boy replied.

"Take a look at one of his paws," Travis suggested. "That cat's been walking a long time."

"And his hair's matted up with sandspurs," another boy said, leaning closer to the cat. "He's been in a field somewhere."

"See, he's told you a lot already, and he isn't even awake yet. Let him rest. Then we'll take a ride back out of town. Maybe we can find the place where those men are holed up."

The boys left Samson in the office. Travis blocked the door with a crate so the cat couldn't escape.

"We'll meet here about three," he said. "It'll be easier riding then."

Samson heard the boys leave and he stirred, but didn't get up. He awoke about one o'clock, ready to be on his way. A quick inspection told him that he was locked in.

He ignored the door and once again tried the upward way. A few quick leaps took him to the old rafters. A broken board gave him access to the outer warehouse. In a few minutes he had slipped into the freedom of the warm summer day.

He paused for a few moments to get his bearings. Then he headed home. At the corner of Main and Tarleton Road, he passed within yards of Mark and Maria Delores. Since Corey had been confined to his house for his negligence in taking care of Cinnamon, Mark and Maria Delores were returning the audio equipment alone. Samson crossed the street in front of them. Mark almost dropped the mike.

"There's Samson!" he yelled.

Maria Delores looked at the dusty cat. Samson heard his name and turned to stare at them. He recognized Mark and came zigzagging back across the street. His purr reverberated in his wide chest as he rubbed against Mark's leg.

"Here, old boy," Mark said gently. He put the equipment back on the bike and lifted the cat. Samson flexed his claws happily.

Mark winced when he saw the raw places on the cat's paws. "Come on, buddy," he said. "Let's get you home."

Their first stop was at Mrs. Wolsiak's house. Inga Wolsiak greeted them with tears of joy. Samson forgot all about the meaning of a cat's dignity and responded like a kitten.

That evening Mrs. Wolsiak insisted on celebrating by inviting the Crimebusters and their parents over for ice cream and cake.

"I'm glad Samson is home safe," Mark said, "but the case isn't closed yet. I'm worried about those dogs. If it's all right, we would like to keep investigating."

"No more night work?" His father's voice was stern.

"No, sir; no more," Mark promised. He turned to Mrs. Wolsiak. "I've been thinking. When Samson is feeling better, I think he could lead us to the dognappers."

"How?"

"Well, Samson was covered with shell dust and sandspurs. I figure that he was held somewhere out of town, like out on old Sandy Flat Road. If we take Samson back down Sandy Flat Road, we can get a general idea of where those dognappers are. And, once in the area, we can use the parabolic mike to locate them."

"From a distance?" Mrs. Conley sounded doubtful.

"Right. And we'll call the police," Mark said quickly. "We won't try to arrest them, or anything like that."

Mrs. Wolsiak was dubious at first about letting the boys take Samson. But since the cat had recovered rapidly, she agreed to the plan.

By Saturday afternoon, everything was set. Maria Delores had fixed a comfortable basket for Samson. Corey had securely strapped the equipment she brought into place. Mark led the way across town.

At Edgewood Trail, Corey hesitated. "Do we have to come this way?"

"Sandy Flat Road is the most logical place for Samson to have been," Mark said. "The shell dust and sandspurs indicate a country road. And he came from this direction."

"What if we run into Travis?" Maria Delores asked.

"We probably will, since he's right over there," Mark said, nodding toward a small grocery store.

Travis swung away from the side of the building when he saw them.

"Hey!" he yelled. "What's going on? How'd you get that cat?"

Mark stopped. "He came home by himself."

"Yeah?" Travis scowled. "Well, I found him first. And he's gonna lead me to my dog. So give him back."

"No, I won't," Mark said. "Mrs. Wolsiak told us to take care of him. But we're planning on using him to find the dognappers too. You can come with us."

Travis's scowl deepened.

Mark didn't try to hold on to Samson. He could tell by the fur rising on the cat's back that Samson felt the tension. Any sudden move, and the cat might take off on his own.

Finally, Travis said, "Okay, but no tricks. I just want my dog."

In uneasy silence, the four pedaled out of town. About five miles out, they passed the turnoff to Colverton.

"Which way?" Mark said, stopping to rest.

"Colverton or Inglewood?" Maria Delores hesitated. "If we go straight ahead, it's ten miles to Inglewood on the point. If we turn left, it's only two to Colverton. What do you think, Travis?"

Travis's reply was cut off as a van approached the intersection. It pulled out and turned toward Inglewood. The van accelerated past them.

"Hey," Travis said. "That's a green van!"

"We're on the right track after all!" said Mark. "Let's go!"

The four pedaled furiously but were unable to keep the van in sight. Finally they stopped, panting.

"Landscaping," Corey said, wheezing. He had been riding a safe distance from Samson, but the dust made him gasp for breath.

"Doesn't matter," Mark said, breathing hard himself. "The dognappers have to turn off the road somewhere. They're surely not going right into Inglewood. Not with the police chief after them. We'll just have to keep an eye out for tracks."

"Well, I'm not going to fold up here," Travis said sharply. "They've got my dog. Come on!"

Corey pulled out a tissue and sneezed several times. Mark and Maria Delores waited. Ahead Travis circled his bike back toward them. "Are you coming or not?"

"It's not them," Corey said between sneezes. "Landscaping. Inglewood Landscaping."

"You mean we're following the wrong truck?" Mark asked. "Hey, Travis! Wait!"

"Let's go, slowpokes!" Travis started to pedal.

Maria Delores and Corey looked at Mark. He shrugged and said, "Okay, so it wasn't the crooks. This direction is still as good as any right now. Let's go!"

Chapter Eleven
Captured!

Mark caught up with Travis. "Wrong van," he told the other boy. "That one was Inglewood Landscaping."

"You want to go back?" Travis asked.

"No," Mark replied. "Let's keep going for a while."

The road unfolded in front of them in a long, gray line. It shimmered in spots where the summer haze made the air dance. Travis set the pace. His legs pumped steadily up and down, and he showed no sign of tiring.

Finally Mark called a halt. "I need a rest," he said, wiping his face with his arm. He looked back at Corey, who had dropped even farther behind. "And I know Corey does. We should have brought some water."

Travis circled impatiently in the road ahead of them. "I thought you guys could ride," he said in disgust.

"We haven't been doing any long distance traveling," Mark said. "Just hold on a minute, Travis. We'll be all right. Corey has trouble with allergies, especially when he's around Samson."

For the first time a grin lightened Travis's face. He rode over to rub the cat behind the ears. Samson lounged over the basket and tipped his head back, purring loudly. "Doesn't like Corey much, does he?"

"No. It's a long story." Mark left Samson with Travis and rode back to help Corey.

Samson stiffened in Travis's arms when Corey rode up with Mark. He laid back his ears and hissed. Corey stopped a safe distance away and pulled out an inhaler.

Travis stopped laughing when he saw that Corey really was having trouble breathing. "Hey," Travis said. "There's no rush. Why don't we take a break? There's a big tree over there in that pasture."

Corey gulped his thanks. They pulled their bikes off the road and crawled through the barbed wire into the pasture. Travis carried Samson and kept ahead of Corey. Maria Delores got the mike out of her basket and carried it carefully.

They all stretched out in the thick green grass. For a while they were silent, listening to the gentle buzzing of insects working in the wild grasses alongside the road. Sea gulls wheeled over from the gulf. A breeze swung through the pasture, tugging at their damp shirts.

"How come you're still looking for the dog-nappers?" Travis asked suddenly. He glanced down at the purring cat sprawled in his arms. "Your case is solved."

"Yours isn't," Mark said. "And others have lost dogs in the last few days." He glanced at Corey, "We almost lost one ourselves."

Travis frowned. "I don't know if I'd bother—not after I found Skeeter."

"Yes, you would," Mark propped himself up on one elbow to look at Travis. "You would because you'd want those men brought to justice. Just like we do."

"You trying to tell me I'm just like you?" Travis's voice held a hostile edge again. "No way. I'm me, Travis Burke, and we Burkes take care of ourselves. We don't need help from anybody."

"Everybody needs help, Travis," Maria Delores said. She sat up, brushing off her arms. "Even you."

"Hey!" he said. "I came to get my dog and that's all." His hands tensed on the cat. Samson slid out of his grasp and stalked away.

"Hey, wait!" Mark leaped up. "Come here, Samson. Come on back."

The cat stopped and looked back over his shoulder. For a moment Mark thought he would return. Then, he darted across the grass.

"Oh, no," Mark moaned. "I promised Mrs. Wolsiak nothing would happen to that cat!"

"Get him!" cried Maria Delores. She and the boys were on their feet immediately. They moved in a running walk after the cat, trying not to alarm him. Samson slipped under the fence on the other side of the pasture and headed over a section of fallen wire.

The detectives followed. Covered with burrs and stung by briars, they stumbled out of the field onto the shell road that bordered it. Their sneakers kicked up puffs of white dust as they trotted after the cat. Samson seemed content to follow the road. He loped along, leaping potholes easily, staying just out of reach.

Fear of losing the cat forced Mark into making a lunge for him. The animal increased his speed smoothly. Mark tripped and fell full length onto the crushed shell of the road.

He raised his head and spat out dirt and shell. He started to scramble to his feet. Then he saw something that made him catch his breath. "Hey, guys!" he called. "Come here!"

The others gave up their hopeless task of catching the cat and trotted back to Mark.

"You hurt, Mark?" Maria Delores asked. He stayed on his hands and knees, probing at something in the road.

"Nope." Mark raised up. "But take a look at what's literally under our noses!"

Travis knelt beside him and inspected the ruts. "Fresh tracks."

"Could be a farm truck," Maria Delores suggested.

Mark motioned toward the field. "The field's unworked, and the pasture's not been used in ages.

If there's a farmhouse down this road, it'll be deserted."

Travis nodded. "Good thinking, Conley," he said. "Let's check it out."

"We can check something right now," Maria Delores said, tapping the mike. "If there are dogs around here, this should pick them up."

Mark agreed. "Let's give it a try."

Maria Delores put on the earphones and pointed the mike toward the east, down the road. She turned slowly, listening.

"What is it?" Mark said impatiently. "What do you hear?"

Maria Delores pulled one earphone away long enough to say, "A farm dog." When Mark reached for the mike, Maria Delores grinned. "Just one."

She tried the west with no results. Then she swept the mike toward the north. Mark saw excitement dawn in her eyes. "Lots of dogs," she said, speaking loudly over a noise the boys couldn't hear.

"Then this road must turn ahead," Mark said, unwilling to give up his theory. "Let's check it out!"

"Aren't we supposed to call the police?" Corey asked.

"Not yet," Travis said. "What proof do we have of anything right now? What would you tell them?"

Mark nodded. "We don't even have a decent suspicion. What would Sheriff Hadley say if we told him we'd heard dogs barking? Besides, Samson has disappeared down that road, and I'm going to get him back."

Corey shrugged. "I guess you're right."

"Then let's stop talking and get going," Travis said.

Sure enough, a few yards ahead the road curved and turned north. The detectives crawled over a gate and followed the road. They came to a long unused yard, overgrown with palmettos, tangled vines, and untrimmed shrubbery.

"Hey," Travis said quietly. "This is the old Talmadge house. I heard some folks used it for a summer place—long time ago. It's been deserted for years." The four crouched behind one of the bushes and stared at the weatherworn house. It sat solidly in the underbrush, enduring in spite of the sagging porch roof, the boarded up windows, and the splintered steps.

"It looks creepy," Corey whispered. "Nobody in his right mind would want to live out here anyway. Let's go."

"Wrong, Corey," Maria Delores whispered back. "Check that out."

The van was barely hidden by the overgrown bushes, but its color blended so well that it was almost unnoticeable.

A movement at the front of the house caught Mark's attention. He groaned, "And look at that!"

Samson emerged from under the broken steps and headed around the side of the house.

"Now what?" Mark squatted down beside Travis. "I promised Dad that we'd only check it out. But now I've got to get that cat back."

"Get down!" Travis said.

The door to the house creaked open. Two men stepped out on the porch.

"It's them!" Corey gasped. "They're the ones who tried to take Cinnamon!"

Mark crouched lower as the men came down the front steps. One man got into the van and backed it around to the porch.

The taller man moved about restlessly, his eyes darting about. "It's about time we got out of here," he said. "This is the weirdest place we've ever worked. Crazies in the house; crazies on the streets!"

"You just let yourself get spooked, Albert," the other man said. He spoke loudly enough to be heard over the barking dogs. "Between this town and Inglewood, we have a good supply for Eldridge. Must be close to three or four thousand dollars in it for us."

"Spooked!" The man called Albert straightened up, visibly outraged. "Some weirdo running around with a razor, a thing floating in the air, and voices from outer space in my ear! You'd be spooked, too, Mick—," he finished weakly as Mick turned around.

"The only thing that is weird around here is you," Mick said roughly. "Now get down here and help me load this van!"

Albert moved reluctantly down the steps. "All I can say," he complained, "is it's a good thing we're pulling out right now. I wouldn't spend another night in this dump."

"Hurry up, then," his partner snapped. "Or we'll be all night loading those dogs."

Mark gave Travis a dismayed look. "We need the police, now," he whispered.

Maria Delores pulled at his arm. "I'll go," she said softly.

Mark nodded. "We'll keep an eye on things here," he whispered back.

Maria Delores crept backward into the tangled grass. The boys watched until she was out of sight.

Then Mark pointed to a sheltering tree and began to creep toward it. The boys understood and followed him. Mark slid under a huge mass of dangling honeysuckle vines.

Travis followed him through and released the springy vines. They swung back, swishing across Corey's face. Corey gasped. Mark grabbed Travis and jerked him into the shadows just as Corey sneezed. Honeysuckle!

"What's that?" Albert spun around.

His partner charged into the clump of vines. Corey sneezed again. And again. Mick hauled him out into the open. Corey stared up at his captor and let loose another series of sneezes.

The man dropped him on the steps in disgust. "A runny-nosed kid! Of all the—this has got to be the worst job we've ever pulled!"

"What're we gonna do with him?" Albert asked.

"That's a good question," his partner said sourly.

Underneath the concealing vines, Mark and Travis stared at each other.

"Take him inside and lock him in the empty room," Mick said. "We'll figure out what to do with him later."

"The empty room?" The thin man's eyes widened.

"Yeah," his partner replied. "If you're right, maybe we won't have to do anything with him."

Albert gave Corey a pitying look. "Come on, kid," he said. "Let's go."

Mark and Travis watched from the shadows of the vines as the man led Corey inside. Mark pressed the light on his watch. He read the numbers in the faint glow.

"It'll take a half hour for Maria Delores to get back to town," he whispered. "And maybe another ten or fifteen minutes for the Sheriff to get here. If they'll stay put that long, we'll be okay."

"And if they don't?" Travis whispered back.

Mark didn't answer.

Inside the house, Albert pushed Corey down in an old chair. Corey sank into its tattered depths, wincing as a broken spring hit his side.

"Here, kid," the man said. "I wouldn't put a dog in that empty room." He giggled. "A dog. Get that, kid?"

Corey glanced around uneasily.

"Don't try anything, kid," his captor said. "Mick's outside. Just sit there and I'll get some twine from the kitchen. You won't move, will you?"

Corey shook his head without speaking.

"Good."

Corey sat stiffly in the chair and listened to the man's movements in the kitchen.

"I told Mick not to leave that door open," Albert fussed. "Garbage spilled everywhere, drawers pulled out, doors left open, junk everywhere—ah, here it is."

He reappeared in the front room, holding a ball of heavy twine. "This ought to hold you," he said.

He folded a length of twine several times, then wound it around Corey's wrists. He did the same to Corey's legs.

"There," he said cheerfully. "You look like a chicken ready to be plucked."

Corey sneezed again.

Albert paused on his way to the door. He looked back at Corey. "Summer cold?"

Corey shook his head. "Allergies."

"You got one of those inhaler things?" Albert asked, looming back over Corey. Corey nodded, and Albert patted the boy's pockets. "Here it is."

He held it for Corey to take a breath, then inspected him. "Don't want to turn you loose . . . Ah!" He separated the lengths of twine around Corey's wrists and retied them, leaving a space between the wrists. Then he looped the twine behind Corey's head, pulling his hands to his face.

"Here," he said, putting the inhaler in Corey's right hand. "That's the best I can do."

Mick appeared at the doorway. "Get a move on, Albert," he snapped.

"Coming," Albert replied sharply. He headed for the door. "Just sit tight," he called back over his shoulder. "And don't waste your breath yelling. There's nobody for miles around."

Corey sneezed.

Chapter Twelve
Any Minute

Corey didn't see Samson until the man went back outside. The cat lay under the couch, watching him. Corey stared back in dismay.

Samson slid out from under the couch in one easy motion. He stalked toward Corey and sat down two feet in front of him. Corey didn't move. He couldn't. He just stared back at the cat.

Samson rumbled deep in his throat and moved toward Corey. Still Corey didn't move. Puzzled, Samson sat back down.

His eyes still fixed on Corey, he lashed his tail threateningly. The boy sat motionless in the old chair, staring back at the cat.

Finally the cat lost interest in his unresponsive prey. He trotted down the hall. Corey sank back into the chair.

Samson's tail disappeared into the empty room just as the front steps creaked again.

"I'll get the dogs ready," Albert said. "I'll be glad to get out of here."

"Put enough in their food to do the job," Mick called. "I don't want them to wake up in the van. But not too much—it's only ten minutes to Colverton and ten more to Eldridge's warehouse."

Outside, Mark turned to Travis. "Eldridge! He's talking about Eldridge Pet Stores! It's a chain of pet shops across the state!"

"Yeah, yeah. Every kid knows about Eldridge Pet Stores. So what?"

"Eldridge is buying the stolen dogs!"

"Not mine, he isn't!" Travis was halfway out of the hiding place before Mark grabbed him.

"Wait!" Mark warned. "Maria Delores and the sheriff'll be here any minute."

Travis sat back. "They'd better be!"

Inside the house, Samson climbed up the mattress and jumped into the ceiling. He stepped along the rafter to look down at the milling dogs.

The cat maneuvered around so he could see the bowls on the floor. They were empty. His stomach rumbled. The garbage can had yielded nothing worthwhile. He settled down to wait for feeding time.

About ten minutes later, Albert opened the door just far enough to shove in a pan of food. The dogs charged forward eagerly. They jumped and leaped over each other in their frantic efforts to get at the small pan of food.

Samson was on his feet in a flash. He dropped down into the mob of dogs, slashing about with all claws extended. The surprised dogs scattered. One of the larger dogs crashed against the door. It swung completely open, knocking Albert into the hall. He lay on the floor, half-stunned as the door bounced against the wall.

The dogs poured out the door. Albert fell back as a Great Dane whipped past him. The dogs scattered in all directions—over the furniture, down the hall.

They flowed in a tangled mass into the kitchen. Stumbling over each other, they raced back out. Corey pulled his bound legs up into the rocker. He closed his eyes. Only once did he try to duck. That was when the Great Dane charged over the rocker as if it weren't even there.

The sound of the commotion carried clear out into the yard. Mick ran up the steps and yanked the front door open to yell at Albert. The dogs leaped over and under him and out into the yard.

"Can't you do anything right?" Mick shouted. He turned around and ran after the dogs.

Albert crawled to his feet and staggered into the front room. His mouth worked but no sounds came out.

"Out, out!" Mick yelled. "Get the kid and let's go!"

Albert picked up Corey and hurried with him to the van. Then he went back to help Mick.

"Don't just stand there," yelled Mick. "Half the county will be up here in a minute!"

Albert and Mick waded into the pack of dogs and Mick snatched up a Yorkshire terrier and a poodle. He tossed them into the back of the van with Corey. "We might as well get something out of this mess!"

The poodle jumped out as Mick snared a golden retriever and hefted it into the van. "Albert!" Mick roared. He caught the poodle by the leg. Turning, he found himself facing a Doberman. Mick dropped the

yelping poodle and swung up into the van, slamming the doors behind him.

"They're getting away!" Travis shouted, leaping up.

Mark was right behind him.

The engine started as Travis and Mark charged out of the bushes. Mick gave them an exasperated look as the van roared past them. "More kids!" he said bitterly.

"Come on," Travis shouted. "Let's get our bikes!"

"Wait," Mark replied, running to the porch. "We'll never catch them, but we know where they are going."

"Colverton?"

"Yeah." Mark ran into the house. Samson was still eating from the pan of food.

"Forget him," Travis said. "He'll be out like a light in a minute. We can pick him up later."

"I need a pen or something to write with," Mark said, hastily searching the kitchen. "We have to leave a message for the sheriff."

He found a pencil stub in a drawer and ripped up a grocery bag. He scribbled on the torn paper: Colverton—Eldridge warehouse. Travis was whistling and calling for Skeeter. Mark rushed to the front door, and stuck the paper between the door and the doorjamb. When he slammed the door shut, the paper fluttered in the breeze.

Travis came around the corner. "Skeeter's not here!"

"They might have sent him off with another shipment," Mark said, dropping the pencil. "Let's get them!"

Chapter Thirteen
In Pursuit

The boys headed for the road. They charged through the tangled grass of the fields. They slid and rolled under the dangling barbed wire. They pounded through the thick pasture grass.

Their bikes still lay propped on the bank of the road, along with Corey's.

Travis took off.

"Hey!" Mark said. "Maybe we should wait on the Sheriff!"

"He can catch up with us," Travis yelled back. "Come on!"

Mark pushed off. It took every bit of energy he had left to catch up with Travis. The two boys turned at the Colverton road, and they rode silently toward Colverton, pushing hard.

A mile down the road, they came to a crossroads gas station. Mark flagged Travis down. "Phone," he said breathlessly.

Travis nodded. The two boys crunched onto the gravel shoulder and fished in their pockets for change. They pooled what they had and counted out seventy-two cents.

Mark called first. His mother didn't waste any time discussing the situation. When Mark hung up, he knew his father would be in Colverton soon— maybe before he got there.

Travis made his call. "Aunt Jan won't be home," he said. The phone rang and rang. "Okay, I told you I could take care of myself, anyway." He looked at Mark. "Do we go on, or wait here?"

"We go on," Mark said. "Corey must be scared stiff."

They reached Colverton fifteen minutes later and found the warehouse in an area of condemned buildings. It was old and apparently deserted. The boys parked their bikes and inspected the building.

"Reckon we got it wrong?" Mark whispered. "I thought sure Dad would be here by now, or at least the Sheriff. Maria Delores left a long time ago."

"You can't depend on other people," Travis said. "See that broken window up there?"

Mark opened his mouth to reply, but Travis was already running toward the building. Mark followed.

At the back of the building, they found the fire escape. Travis leaped and caught the folded end. He and Mark pulled it down. Then they crept up the metal steps.

The door at the top had a strong, working lock. Mark hung over the edge of the railing to peer through the broken window Travis had seen from below. He heard a faint bark from the depths of the building.

"They're here," he said. "And we can get in this way."

Travis nodded. They edged cautiously across the railing. Mark swung in the window first and Travis followed. Mark stepped over empty paint cans and a stack of old drop cloths. Travis landed quietly behind him. They stared around at the dimly lit space. Dusty boxes towered nearly eight feet on either side of them.

"It's a storage loft," Mark whispered.

Just as Travis opened his mouth to answer, they heard a voice. Using the boxes for cover, they moved toward the edge of the loft.

Mark squeezed past a row of boxes and crouched by the railing of the loft. Right below him was the van. The back door gaped open. Corey lay on the van floor, gagged and tied.

The two men paced in front of the van, leading the terrier and retriever on leashes.

"What'll we do now?" Travis asked.

"I don't know," Mark said. "We can't get to Corey without being seen. We'll have to wait for Dad."

"Will he be able to handle these two?" Travis sounded skeptical.

"My dad can do anything," Mark said firmly.

The boys edged into a position where they could see and hear what was being said, then settled down to wait. Albert paced nervously back and forth. His footsteps echoed hollowly in the quiet.

"I wish I had never come to this town," he complained. "Do you think something may have followed us here?"

Mark nudged Travis as the man glanced nervously back into the shadows of the warehouse.

"What followed us here?" asked Mick.

"That thing," Albert said. "It nearly knocked the door off the hinges. I tell you, it slung me clear into the hall!"

"You let the dogs jump you."

"Then you explain the razor marks on the mattress and those awful wails in the night," Albert whined. "And the garbage thrown all over the kitchen. What on earth would do that?"

Mark exchanged a puzzled glance with Travis. There had been nothing else in that house except Samson.

Mark began to grin. A torn mattress. Spilled garbage. Spooked dogs. The facts clicked through his mind. And they added up to one big cat—Samson.

"That tall man is afraid of Samson," he whispered to Travis. "But he doesn't know it's Samson. He doesn't know what caused all the strange things that happened to them here. Sounds like he's awful superstitious!"

He sat back and thought for a minute. Finally he whispered, "I know how we can fix them. We passed some things on the way in that would come in handy right now. Let's take a look in the back of the loft!"

Chapter Fourteen
Cover the Back

Mark and Travis backtracked until they reached the drop cloths. They checked three until Mark found one that was worn and softened enough for his purpose.

He held it up, letting it flap gently. Understanding dawned in Travis's eyes. "Are you thinking what I'm thinking?" he asked, grinning.

"Uh-huh," Mark replied. "Samson has that guy Albert spooked, literally. The man is scared out of his mind already. If we attach this cloth to the pulley that swings down from the loft to the warehouse floor—"

"They're right below it!" Travis nodded. "Albert'll run like a rabbit!"

"But Mick won't," Mark said. "And he has a gun."

"Scared?" Travis asked.

"Sure, who wouldn't be?" Mark replied. "And remember, I promised Dad that we would only do surveillance—no capture stuff. That's why I called him on the way here. He'll be here in a few minutes."

"Then why bother with this?"

"Because Mick has that gun," Mark said. "And Dad will probably come in the front. That's just the way he is. We're going to cover the back."

"You've really thought it through," Travis said, reluctant admiration in his voice. "I would've just charged right in."

"We've been through this once or twice before," Mark said, remembering the time Sheriff Hadley had found him trapped, hanging upside down in a tree.

They worked silently. First they draped the cloth over a rod and tied the rod onto the hook of the pulley. Then they secured the pulley to a length of rope so the pulley could be released from the side.

"Mick will probably shoot at the cloth," Mark whispered. "We'll have to get out of range."

Travis nodded. Below them, the men still paced, impatience evident in their restless movements. The boys finished their work and moved back into the nest of boxes. "Think Albert's really gonna buy it?" Travis sounded worried.

"Sure. Even Mick hasn't been able to talk him out of what he thinks he saw," Mark said. He settled back against a box to wait.

Down below, even Albert had fallen silent.

Car tires crunched on the shell road outside.

Travis and Mark crawled to the edge of the loft and peered over.

The garage door began to lift slowly, flooding the warehouse with sunlight. Mark shrank back, almost tripping over Travis.

"Who is it?"

"Eldridge, I think," Mark whispered.

A dark figure, silhouetted against the light, stopped the door. He got back into a Mercedes Benz and drove into the warehouse. The car stopped and the man got out.

"It's about time you got here," Mick said, looking at his watch. "I phoned you from the crossroads fifteen minutes ago. Let's get moving. We've got to get out of town."

"This all you have?" The man pointed at the two leashed dogs.

"Yeah. It's a long story." Mick sounded angry. "Just pay us for these two and the other shipment, and we'll be on our way."

Mark touched Travis's arm as three shadows darted swiftly across the sunlit space and into the shelter of the warehouse. Two wore uniforms, the other a suit.

"Get into place," Mark whispered.

Below, the men continued to argue. Eldridge began to count out money.

"More," Mick snarled. "We had expenses on this job, see?"

"But just two dogs. That hardly—"

A bump from the window behind the boys sent them spinning around. "Maria Delores," Mark exclaimed. "Quiet! You nearly scared me to death!"

"What's going on?" She crept up to them, almost tripping over the coil of rope.

Travis scowled at her. "How did you find us?"

"I came with the others, silly," she whispered.

"Then why couldn't you have waited in the car like a good little girl?"

Maria Delores leaned against his shoulder and smiled. Travis lost his balance. As he scrambled onto his knees, muttering, she took his place beside Mark. Travis glared at her and regained his hold on the rope. Maria Delores crept to the edge of the loft and peered over.

"You owe us two thousand for this operation," Mick was saying. "It's not our fault it went sour. Are you planning to back out on us?"

Eldridge stepped back. "Now, Mick," he said, "take it easy. We can work something out, I'm sure."

A man's voice boomed from the shadows. "Don't bet on it! Drop that gun and put your hands up!"

Mick whirled and fired at the voice. The bullet echoed in the huge building.

"Now!" Mark yelled.

Travis yanked hard on the rope.

The pulley shuddered and squeaked. It separated from its moorings with a high, shrieking wail of rusting machinery. Albert stared up at it, then leaped away from the other two men.

Something white swooped out of the darkness. It swung toward them in a curving arc. Albert yelled and ran for the door. "Don't shoot! Don't shoot!" he shouted. "I give up."

Mick turned toward the onrushing attacker and emptied his gun at it. When bullets seemed to pass right through the swooping white form, Eldridge ran after Albert.

Only Mick stood his ground. The white form reached the end of its arc and swung back to the loft.

Mark groaned. "What now?"

"I got it! I got it!" muttered Maria Delores.

Too late, Mark tried to grab her. She hooked her legs over the railing and swung down to intercept the cloth on the pulley. For an instant she held it, getting her aim. When she released it, the pulley headed straight for Mick.

He held the empty gun tightly, ready to strike the intruder. The gun handle swished through the rotten cloth as the first folds enveloped the waiting man.

Thud. The iron hook of the pulley grazed Mick's head. Mick crumpled to the floor.

"Yahoo!" Mark and Travis clapped one another on the shoulder. "We did it!"

Maria Delores swung back into the loft. "We?" she said, black eyebrows raised like bird's wings.

"Yeah, we," Travis said, pounding her on the back. "All of us!"

"You kids get down from there!" Sheriff Hadley's voice sounded like thunder.

"Mark!" It was his dad's courtroom voice. "Come here!"

"Oops," Mark said softly. "I think we're in trouble."

He and Travis, followed by a quiet Maria Delores, climbed down the ladder to the waiting men. The deputy was leading Albert and Mr. Eldridge away. Mick still lay stretched out on the floor of the warehouse.

"Hey! Where's Skeeter?" Travis yelled at Albert. "Where's my dog?"

Albert stared at him.

"Hold on, Son," one of the deputies pulled Travis away. "If you're missing a dog, we'll find him when we sort this business out."

"Speaking of business, I thought I told you to stay out of *police* business—" said Sheriff Hadley.

"Mark, you promised—," Mr. Conley stopped. "Maria Delores, I thought you were waiting in the car!"

"But, Dad—" Mark was interrupted by thumping on the side of the van.

"Hold on, Corey," Mark said. "We're coming."

The men helped release the tired boy. He struggled to his feet, then sat down abruptly as his legs began to fold under him.

"Here," Mr. Conley said, "let's get him into my car."

At the car, Mr. Conley hesitated. Clearly visible was a huge cat, pawing at the air freshener that hung from the rear-view mirror.

Mr. Conley swung around to the sheriff's car. It was obviously already full, and the deputy had gone back for Mick.

"I'm sorry, Corey," he said. "We found Samson in the deserted house, asleep on the floor. I'm afraid we'll have to keep him in the car with us."

"No problem," Corey gasped as they settled him in the back.

Samson leaped up on the back of the seat to inspect Corey. The two stared at each other for a long minute. Neither budged. Then Samson lost interest in the boy and returned to his game with the dangling freshener.

"Come on, Travis," Mr. Conley said. "We'll follow them back."

"He'd better still have my dog," Travis said as he slid into the back with Maria Delores and Corey.

"From what I understand, they're all in Eldridge's Sarasota warehouse. None of them have been sent to pet shops yet. We should be able to pick him up tomorrow," Mr. Conley said. "Let's go, Mark."

Chapter Fifteen
Crimebusters, Inc.

Two weeks later, the friends met in the garage loft. Travis rode up, followed by Skeeter, his long-legged Irish setter. Mark met him at the door, and Travis handed him a sign.

Mark held it up. "Crimebusters, Inc.," he read out loud. "It's great, Travis. I didn't know you could paint this good. It really looks professional!"

"My uncle helped me," Travis said. "I thought it would look good over the door."

"So we're in business again," said Mark. After they had driven home that night, he'd been worried that the Crimebusters might never be allowed to take another case. But then they'd explained their actions to the council—made up of all the parents including Travis's aunt and uncle.

While the detectives had waited uneasily in the Conleys' living room, the eight people responsible for them conferred in the study. But finally the "jury" had announced that they had indeed been responsible in their actions, though circumstances had forced them into what the parents called "dangerous situations."

The equipment used in the case had been returned to Uncle Ramon in perfect order. Mr. Conley had been impressed by their care of the complicated electronic equipment. Since he was concerned about the need for the detectives and their parents to keep in touch, he had suggested using part of the reward money for communications equipment. The others had agreed. Best of all, a grateful dog owner had donated a computer for their use.

The new Crimebusters, Inc., was established in the next few days. First, Mark had suggested that Travis join them, and Corey had agreed. Maria Delores was the one who needed convincing, even though Travis had admitted that, for a girl, she was an all right guy.

But then Travis had turned them down. "I work alone," he had said, looking over their loft. "I don't need all this stuff to solve a case."

Mark had shrugged. "Suit yourself. But we'd like to work with you."

"Sure. Sometime." Travis backed down the ladder.

"How about being an associate?" Maria Delores suggested.

"Associate?"

"Sort of a partner, I guess," she replied.

Travis hesitated. "Well, guess it wouldn't hurt to give it a try."

So at last Crimebusters, Inc., complete with its associate, was open for business. Well, at least, they were open. Since business was restricted in a small town like Boca Cay, not much had come their way since Samson had turned up missing.

Mark and Travis tacked up the sign and went upstairs to join Maria Delores and Corey. Maria Delores was setting up a profit and loss statement on the new computer. Samson stretched out on the floor near the edge of the loft, licking his paws and watching the Irish setter down in the garage. Corey was checking out the communications system.

"You know," he said, "we can pick up just about anything on this. Listen!"

A series of crackles and squawks sent Samson charging up in alarm. The cat missed his footing and tumbled over the edge of the loft. He landed upright two inches from the dog's nose and streaked out of the garage, hair on end.

Mark and Travis laughed, but they stopped short when a strange voice whispered into the room.

"Omega here. Meeting k12, a9. 2400. SORBA secured."

The reply was just as secretive. "SeaGo9. ASC."

Then static wiped out the rest.

"What was that, Conley?" Travis asked. He glanced at Mark.

Mark's eyes were focused on something neither he nor they could see. "You know, that sounded like a secret meeting. Almost like a spy contact. What if—"

"Uh-oh." Maria Delores grinned at Travis. "Here we go again!"